SCOOBY-DOO!

BEGINNER MYSTERIES

STONE ARCH BOOKS
a capstone imprint

Published in 2017 by Stone Arch Books, A Capstone Imprint
1710 Roe Crest Drive, North Mankato, Minnesota 56003
www.mycapstone.com

Library of Congress Cataloging-in-Publication Data
Cataloging-in-publication information is on file with the
Library of Congress.
ISBN: 978-1-4965-4769-9 (library binding)
ISBN: 978-1-4965-4773-6 (paperback)
ISBN: 978-1-4965-4777-4 (eBook PDF)

Editorial Credits:
Editor: Alesha Sullivan
Designer: Brann Garvey
Art Director: Nathan Gassman
Media Researcher: Wanda Winch
Production Specialist: Katy LaVigne
Design Elements:
Warner Brothers design elements, 1, 4-8, 106-112
The illustrations in this book were created by Scott Jeralds

Printed and bound in the United States of America.
010400F17

SCOOBY-DOO!

BEGINNER MYSTERIES

SKELETON CREW SHOWDOWN

by Michael
Anthony Steele

illustrated by
Scott Jeralds

TABLE OF CONTENTS

MEET MYSTERY INC.

SCOOBY-DOO

SKILLS: Loyal; super snout
BIO: This happy-go-lucky hound avoids scary situations at all costs, but he'll do anything for a Scooby Snack!

SHAGGY ROGERS

SKILLS: Lucky; healthy appetite
BIO: This laid-back dude would rather look for grub than search for clues, but he usually finds both!

FRED JONES, JR.

SKILLS: Athletic; charming
BIO: The leader and oldest member of the gang. He's a good sport — and good at them, too!

DAPHNE BLAKE

SKILLS: Brains; beauty
BIO: As a sixteen-year-old fashion queen, Daphne solves her mysteries in style.

VELMA DINKLEY

SKILLS: Clever; highly intelligent
BIO: Although she's the youngest member of Mystery Inc., Velma's an old pro at catching crooks.

CHAPTER ONE

READY TO SET SAIL

The Mystery Inc. gang unloaded their suitcases from the Mystery Machine. The calls of seagulls filled the salty air.

Daphne stretched and then pulled out a long handle from her purple suitcase. "I can't remember the last time we had a vacation."

"That's because crooks don't take vacations," said Velma. She pulled on her orange backpack. "And there's always a mystery to solve."

Shaggy lifted a large green duffle bag onto his shoulder. "Like, great idea, Fred. A vacation at sea sounds like fun."

"Don't thank me," replied Fred. "You can thank my friend, Greg Hibbard." Fred picked up his own suitcase. "He's the one who invited us to spend time on his new ship."

Scooby-Doo led the way as the gang walked toward the docks. The wooden walkways crisscrossed into the bay.

The docks were lined with all kinds of parked *watercraft*. There were sailboats, motorboats, and many large, fancy ships. The showy ships were expensive boats that looked like small cruise ships. They had shiny paint jobs, lots of big windows, and were much taller than the other boats.

"Which one belongs to your friend?" asked Velma.

Fred shook his head. "I don't know. Greg said we would know when we saw it."

The gang continued to walk between rows and rows of parked ships.

"Fred!" called a voice. "Over here!"

Everyone looked around to see who was calling. Daphne finally spotted him. "Is that your friend?" she asked Fred.

Daphne pointed to a man standing atop the biggest, fanciest ship they had ever seen. It was almost the size of a real cruise ship.

Fred waved up at the man.

"Greg?"

Greg waved them forward.

"Come on aboard!"

Fred turned back to the others. "I guess this is …" He stopped talking. Everyone was gone.

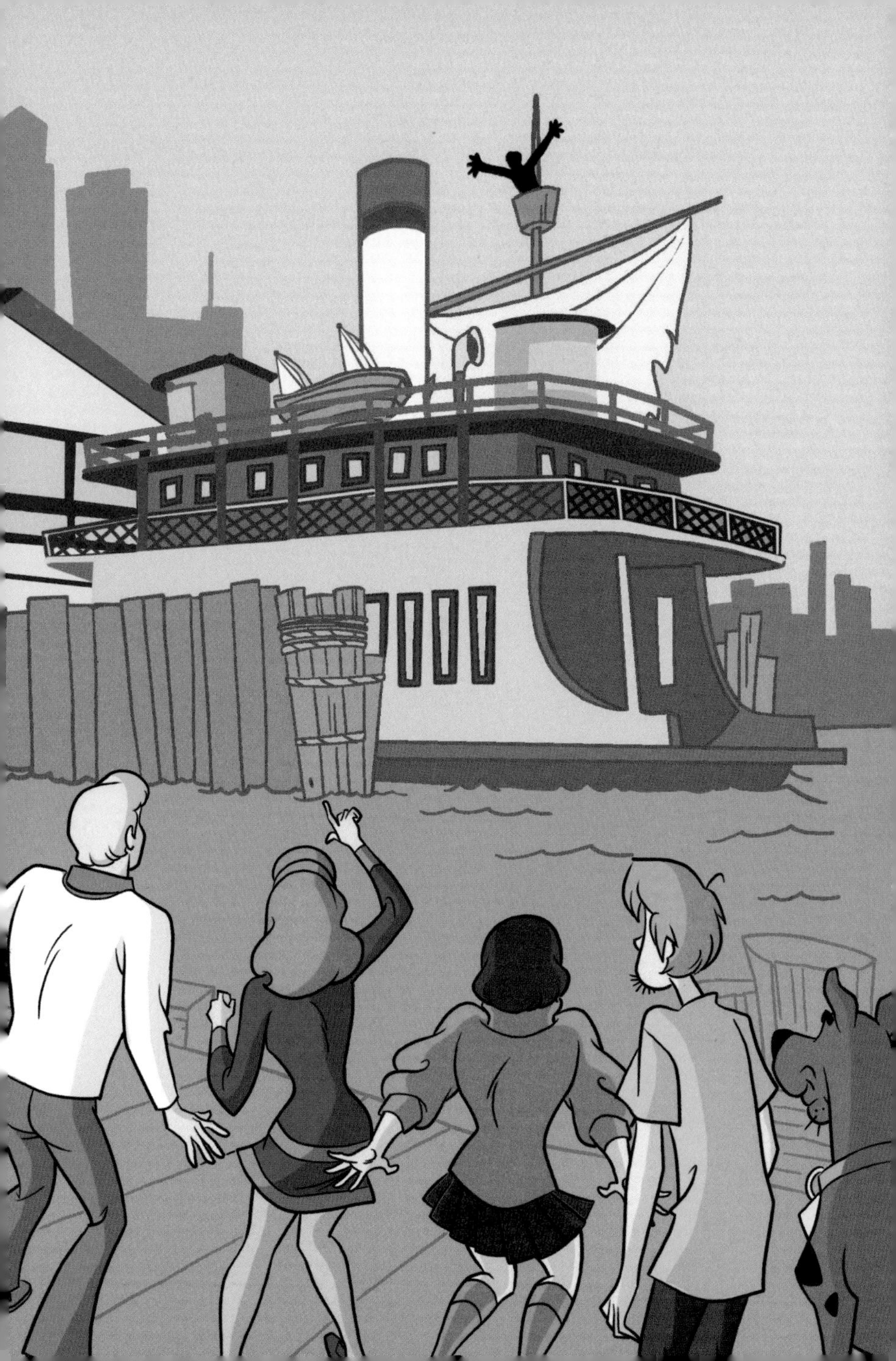

The rest of the Mystery Inc. gang was running up the ramp leading to the ship.

By the time Fred caught up with the others, Daphne and Velma were already laying in lounge chairs. A waiter stood between them, taking their drink orders. Meanwhile, Shaggy and Scooby-Doo stood next to another waiter with napkins tied around their necks.

"So, like, where is the buffet?" asked Shaggy.

Scooby-Doo raised an eyebrow. "Ris it … rall you can eat?"

Suddenly, a large man wearing swim trunks and a big gold necklace charged onto the deck. "What are you kids doing on my ship?!!"

"Your ship?" asked Fred. "But my friend, Greg..."

The man didn't let Fred finish. He raised his sunglasses and looked around. "SECURITY!" he shouted.

THUD!

They gang landed in a heap on the dock. The security men then flung their luggage after them.

Shaggy just got to his feet as his duffel bag slammed into him. He tumbled back along the wooden dock.

"Like, what kind of friend do you have, Fred?" asked Shaggy.

Fred got to his feet and rubbed his head. "I don't know."

Everyone looked up to see Greg still standing atop the large ship. Greg threw his hands up. "What are you doing, Fred?"

Just then, the big ship pulled away from the dock. To everyone's surprise, Greg stayed in place. He wasn't standing on the big ship at all. Instead, he stood atop the highest deck on the ship behind it. It only looked as if he had been standing on the big fancy ship.

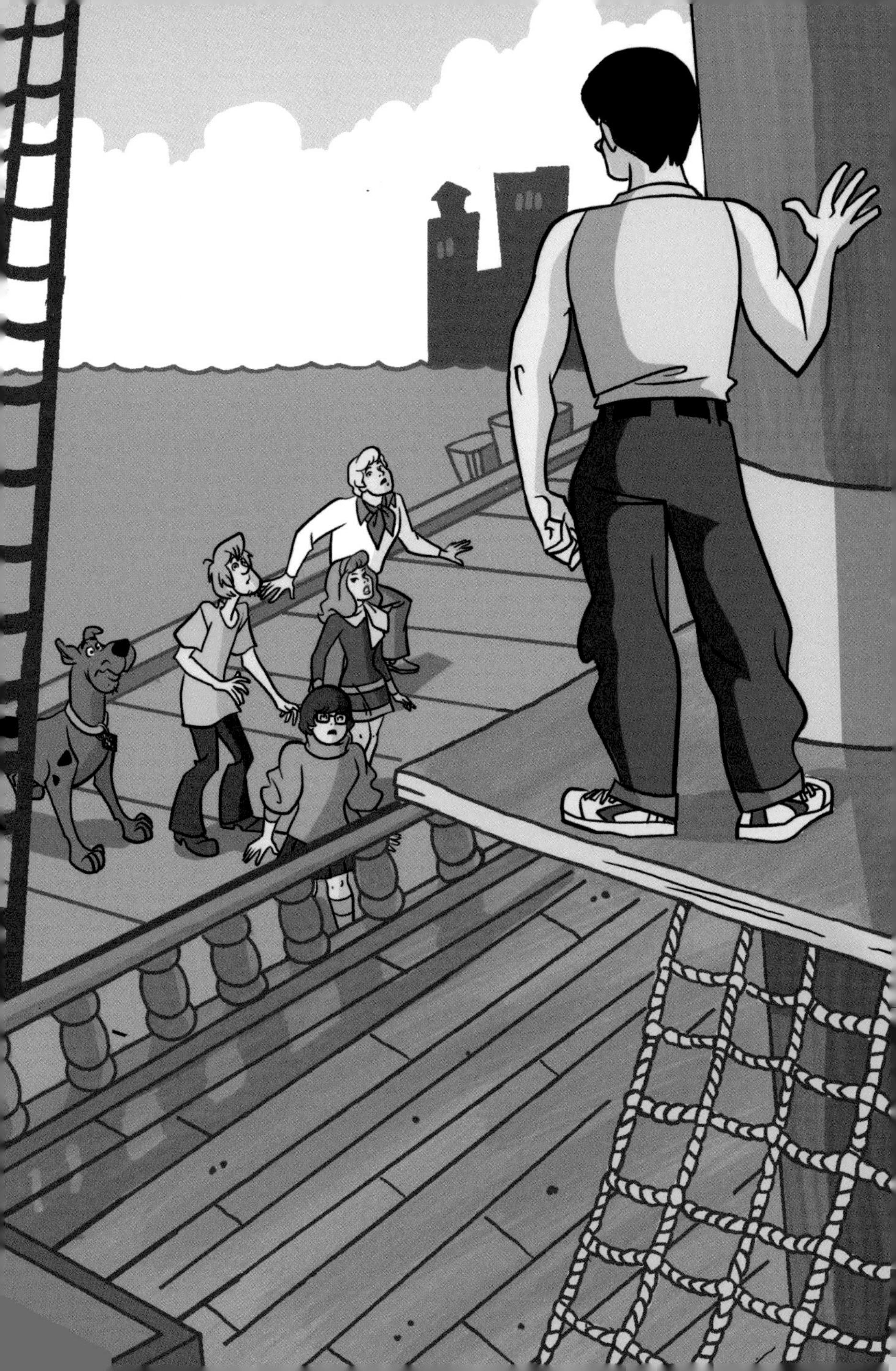

"Wait a minute…" said Velma. "That's your friend's ship?"

Everyone's jaws dropped. Greg stood on the deck of an old, run-down, rickety … pirate ship!

CHAPTER TWO

SOME VACATION

"Careful, everyone," warned Greg. "Watch your step."

Fred was the last to walk up the thin, wobbly *plank* of wood. Once he was aboard the *vessel*, he introduced the rest of the gang. Then everyone looked around the ship. Chipped paint covered the railings. *Tattered* sails flapped in the breeze above them. And the deck was made up of cracked and rotted boards.

Fred rubbed his chin. "Greg, when you invited us to stay on your new ship, I expected something, uh… less…"

"Old," finished Daphne.

"You know?" asked Velma. "The opposite of new?"

"Well, it's new to me," said Greg. "Besides, this was a once-in-a-lifetime chance to be the owner of a real pirate ship." Greg spread his arms wide. "Welcome aboard *The Salty Dog*!"

The Mystery Inc. gang stared blankly at him.

Greg led them toward the front of the ship. "Come on. Let me show you the masthead."

"Rasthead?" asked Scooby.

"That's what they call the carved *statue* on the front of old sailing ships," explained Velma.

"That's right," said Greg. "And this masthead is a wooden statue of none other than the captain of this ship — Angus Grimm!"

Everyone leaned over the railing to look at the masthead. It was a statue of an angry bearded man with a patch over one eye.

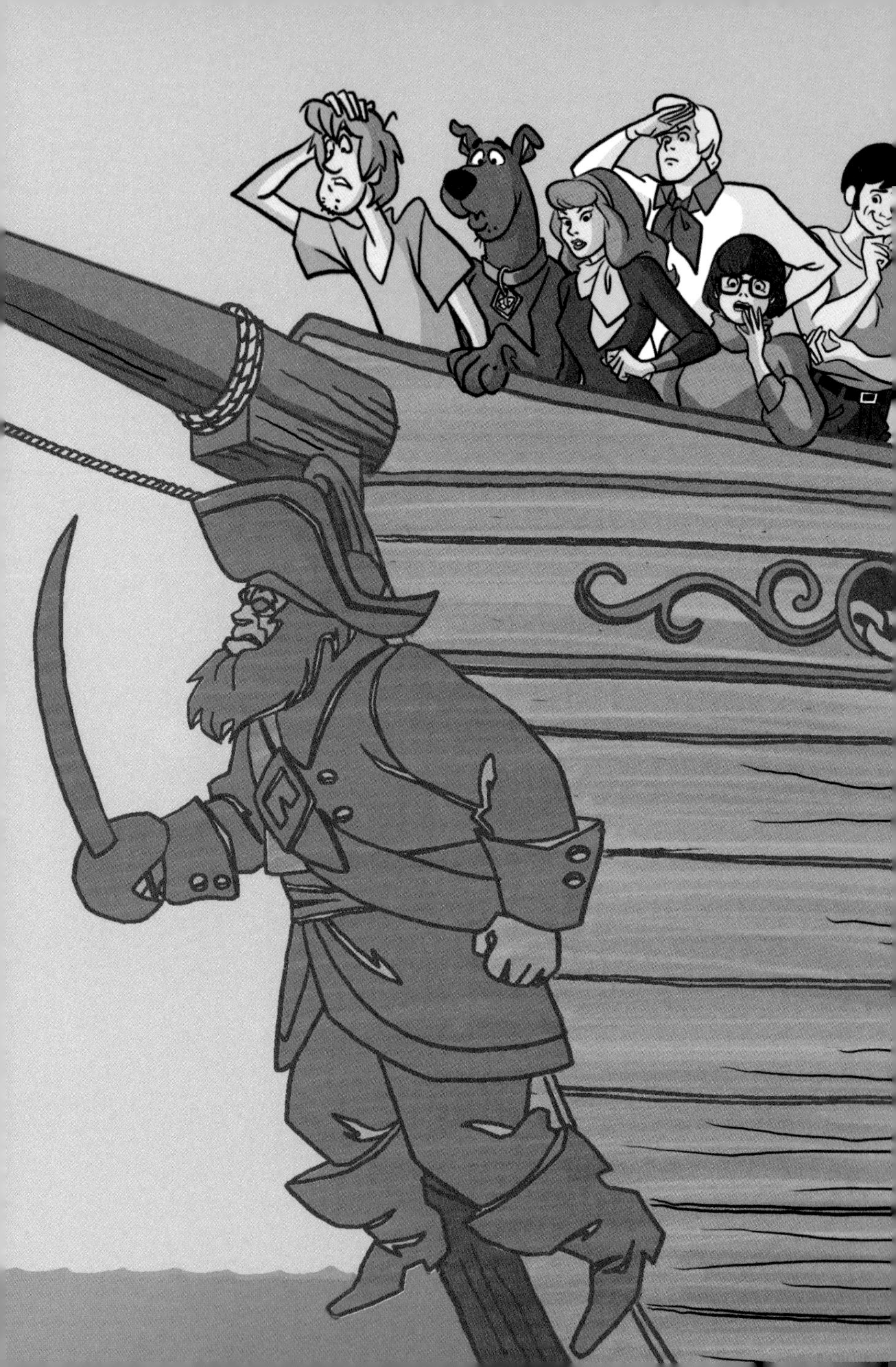

"Now I remember," said Velma. "Angus Grimm was a famous pirate."

Shaggy shivered at the sight of the frowning statue. "Like, he doesn't look like a nice person."

"He wasn't," said Velma. "He was one of the nastiest pirates around."

"And this was his ship," said Greg. "Or what's left of it. I'm going to create a floating Angus Grimm *museum*!"

Greg gave the gang a tour of the ship. He showed them the captain's quarters with its old desk and tattered maps. He led them through the cannon deck. Rows of rusty cannons poked out of openings in the sides of the ship.

He even showed them the brig. It was a special jail on the ship for locking up prisoners.

Greg led them down a long hallway. "I think you all will be perfect to help fix up the ship." He pointed to the strand of light bulbs hanging from the ceiling. "I even have work lights ready to go."

"You know, Greg, we're supposed to be on vacation," explained Fred.

"And when we're not on vacation, we solve mysteries," said Velma. "We're not a work crew."

Greg stopped the tour.

"Fred told me all about you. And I think the Mystery Inc. gang would be perfect to help." Greg pointed at Fred. "Fred's a hard worker, good with his hands, building all those traps," said Greg.

Fred nodded. "That's true, I guess."

"Velma will be a big help with the history," Greg continued. "Making sure we get everything right."

Velma grinned. "You got me there."

Greg pointed at Daphne. "Daphne will be in charge of painting. I hear she's great at matching colors."

Daphne smiled. "It's a gift."

Shaggy put his hands on his hips.

"Wait a minute, buddy boy. I don't know what Fred's told you about me. But there's nothing you can say that'll make me want to spend my vacation on a creepy old pirate ship."

Scooby-Doo crossed his arms. "Reah. Rhat he said."

Greg grinned and opened a nearby door. The cold room was full of fruit, vegetables, and hanging strands of sausages. "Did I mention that this ship has a fully loaded food locker?"

Shaggy drooled. "Like, you had me at food."

Greg finished the rest of the tour and showed them to their rooms.

After a nice dinner, everyone went to sleep. They wanted to be rested for all the hard work the next day.

Early the next morning, Shaggy tossed and turned. He wasn't used to sleeping in a droopy *hammock* like people did on old sailing ships. When he tried to climb out, he flew out of the hammock and hit the floor.

THUMP!

Shaggy rubbed his head. "Like, sorry if I woke you, Scoob."

Scooby-Doo didn't wake up. He continued to snore as he rocked back and forth in his own hammock.

"I left my pillow in the Mystery Machine," Shaggy said to himself. "Maybe that will help."

The sun was beginning to rise as Shaggy climbed the stairs and stepped onto the deck. He sleepily walked toward the plank of wood leading to the docks. But when he stepped over the edge, the plank wasn't there. The ship was no longer tied to the dock.

Shaggy turned and tried to run back to the deck. His legs kicked and kicked, but he didn't go anywhere. Instead, he dropped like a stone.

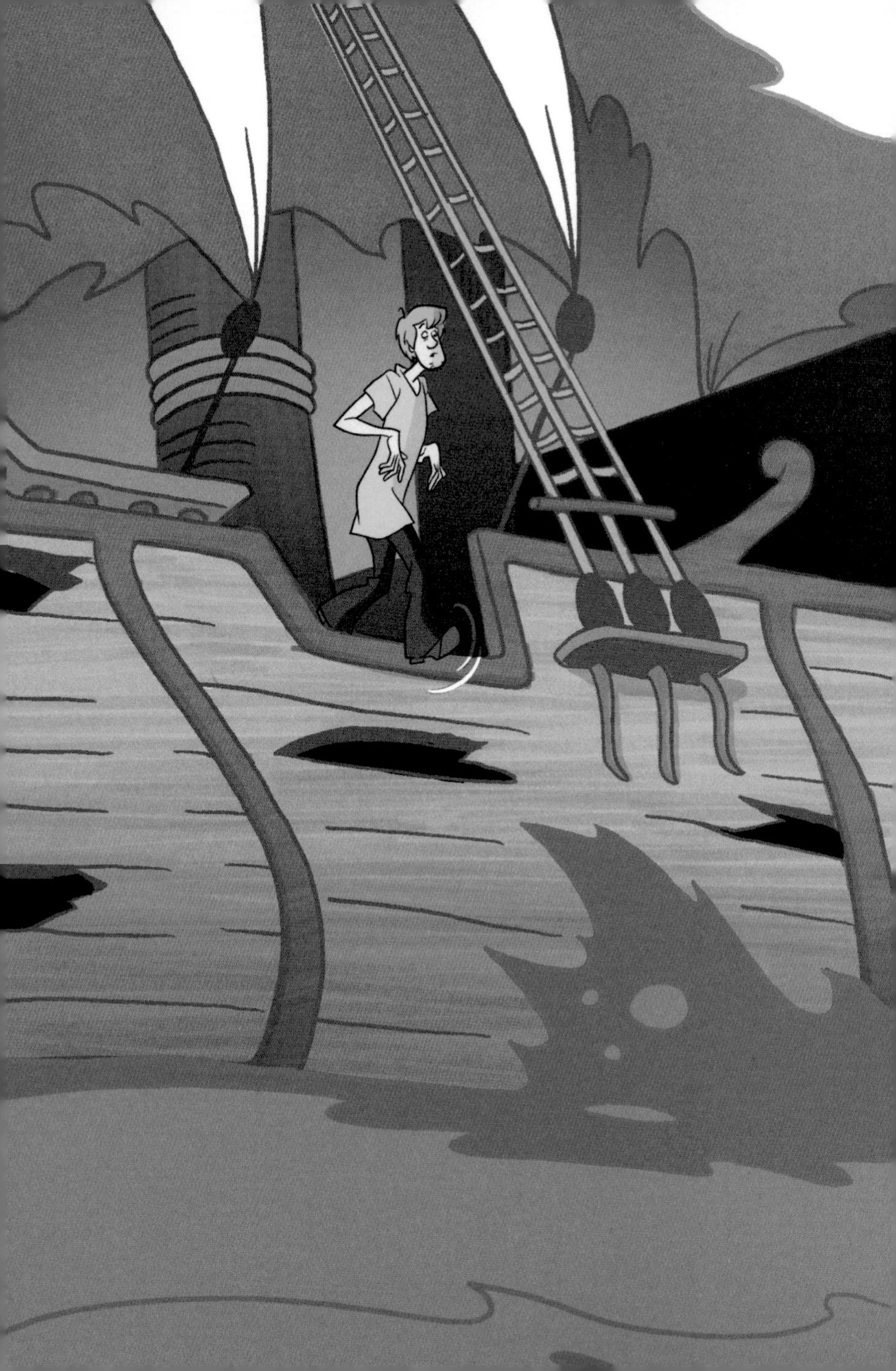

SPLASH!

Shaggy dog-paddled to stay afloat. "Like, man overboard! Help!!!"

CHAPTER THREE

HARD DAY'S WORK

"Okay, gang, one more time," said Fred. "One, two, three ... pull!"

Everyone tugged the large rope. As they did, Shaggy appeared at the railing. He landed and blew a stream of seawater out of his mouth.

"Like, thanks," said Shaggy. "I didn't plan on an early morning swim."

Greg rushed forward and threw
a blanket over Shaggy's shoulders.
"I don't know how this happened,"
admitted Greg. "I made sure the ship
was tied off before we went to sleep."

Velma looked around. There was no
land in sight. "Well, it's not tied off
now. We're floating in the middle of
the sea."

Scooby-Doo reached over the side of the ship. He pulled up the end of a thick rope.

"Rook at the rope," said Scooby. "A rue!"

Fred examined the end of the rope. "It is a clue. This rope has been cut."

"It looks like vacation is over," said Velma. "And we have a mystery to solve."

"Do you know anyone who would want to let your ship drift away from shore?" asked Daphne.

"I have no idea," replied Greg. "But the ship isn't ready to sail. We'll have to fix it up before we can make it back to land."

"Then we better save the mystery for later," said Fred, "and get to work repairing this ship."

Everyone spent the rest of the day working on the old pirate ship. Fred and Velma stitched together tons of cloth to make brand new sails. Greg and Daphne replaced all the old ropes that held up the sails.

Meanwhile, Shaggy and Scooby-Doo repaired old boards around the ship.

By the time the sun began to set, the gang was almost done. While Fred and Velma finished the last sail, Daphne walked by with her arms loaded. She held several paint cans and paintbrushes.

"Where are you going with those?" asked Velma.

"I thought I'd start painting," replied Daphne. "I'm going to begin with that creepy masthead."

"Good idea," said Fred. "We're almost finished with the last sail. Have you seen Greg?"

"Not in a while," said Daphne, as she headed toward the front of the ship.

"I wonder where he is," said Velma.

Scooby-Doo and Shaggy came up on deck. "Like, have you seen Greg?" asked Shaggy.

"I was just asking the same thing," Fred told Shaggy.

"We can't find him anywhere," said Shaggy.

"And we rooked everywhere," added Scooby.

"Like, we were going to reward ourselves with a nice snack," said Shaggy. "But the food locker is locked."

"Hey guys!" shouted Daphne. "You better come look at this!"

Everyone ran to the front of the ship. Daphne leaned over the side and pointed at the masthead. Or, at least, she pointed to where the masthead used to be. Only broken chunks of wood remained.

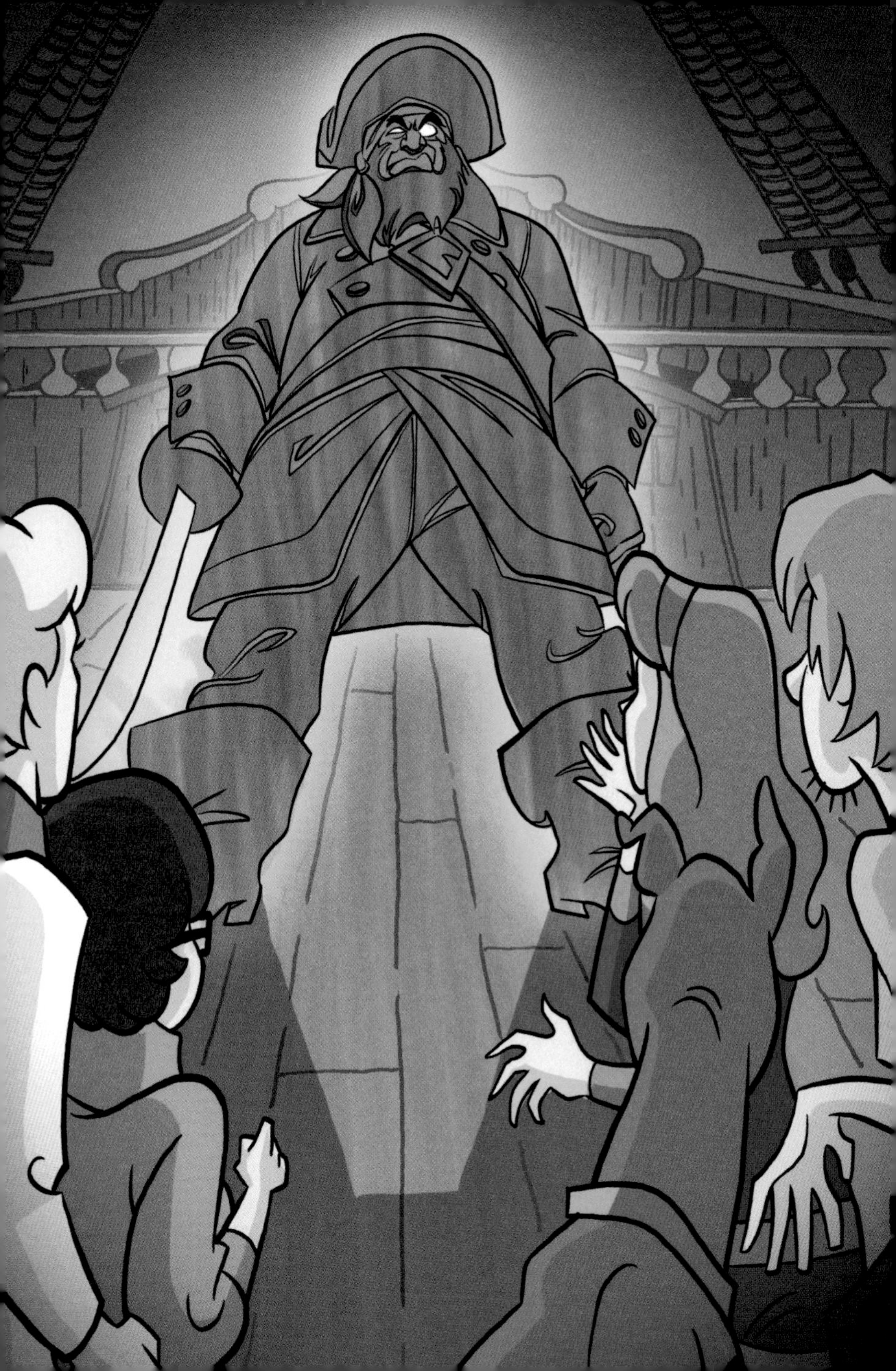

"The masthead is gone," reported Daphne.

Shaggy gulped. "Like, it's almost as if it pulled itself off the front of the boat."

"That's ridiculous, Shaggy," said Velma. "It's just a wooden statue."

Scooby-Doo whimpered and pointed. "Like rat one?"

Everyone turned to see the wooden statue of Angus Grimm standing behind them. He stared blankly with wooden eyes as he slowly drew a long, sharp sword.

CHAPTER FOUR

ATTACK AT SEA

Grrrrrrr!

Angus Grimm growled. Everyone ducked as the pirate swung his sword.

"Run!" shouted Fred.

The group scattered as the pirate raised his sword again. Fred, Velma, and Daphne ran across the deck. With the pirate close behind, they dove through a door leading to the lower decks.

Meanwhile, Shaggy and Scooby-Doo raced toward a nearby lifeboat. It hung just over the side of the ship and was covered with a white cloth. The two friends jumped into the boat and hid under the covering. They hugged each other and trembled with fear.

Tk-tk-tk-tk-tk-tk-tk-tk-tk!

Scooby-Doo was so frightened, his teeth chattered. Shaggy covered Scooby's mouth to stop the noise.

"Like, I feel terrible, Scoob," whispered Shaggy. "Our friends are out there, running for their lives. And we're hiding out like a couple of scaredy-cats."

Scooby nodded. "Rit's kinda rhat we do."

Shaggy took a deep breath. "Well, I'm not going to hide anymore," he said. "There's two of us and only one of him."

Just then, the cloth was ripped away. Angus Grimm stood over them, his sword held high.

Shaggy and Scooby hugged each other and screamed.

"Ahhhhhhhhh!!!"

The pirate swung his sword and cut the ropes holding the lifeboat. It fell and splashed into the water below.

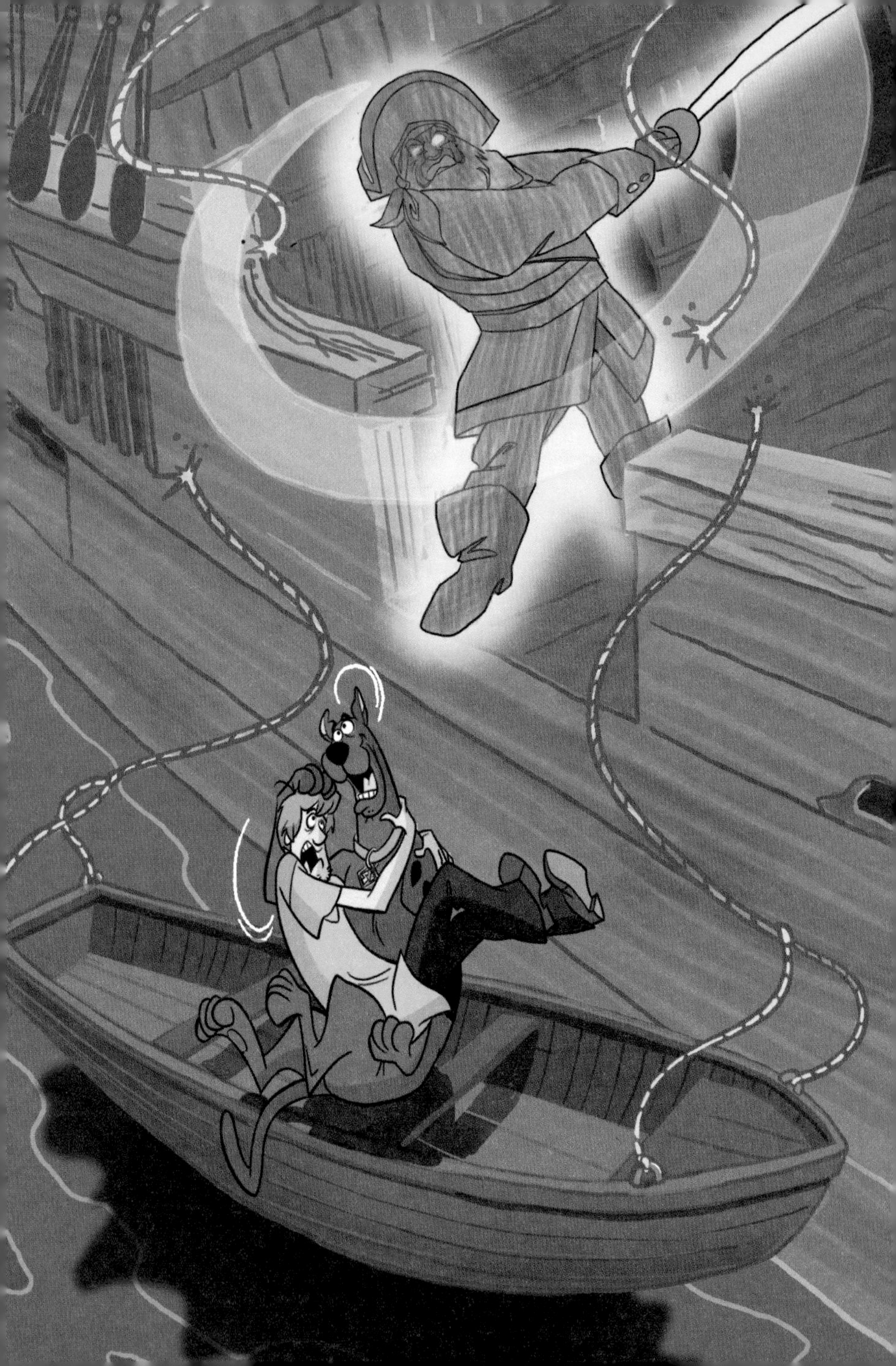

"Like, we're okay, Scoob," said
Shaggy. "He can't get us down here."

The statue of Angus Grimm
growled. He picked up a cannonball
and threw it over the side. Shaggy
ducked as the ball came right at them.

The cannonball crashed through
the bottom of the tiny boat. Water
spurted up through the round hole.
Shaggy quickly covered the hole with
one hand.

Grimm threw another cannonball
at them. The ball crashed through the
bottom of the boat. Shaggy covered
the holes with his hands and feet.

"We gotta do something, Scoob!" shouted Shaggy. "He has more cannonballs, but I'm all out of hole pluggers!"

Scooby-Doo ran to the back of the boat and hung his tail over the side. Scooby's tail began to spin like a *propeller* on an airplane.

Rrrrrrrrrrrrrrr!

The small boat raced around the water. Grimm threw another cannonball, but it missed them completely.

"Great going, pal!" said Shaggy. "Take us to the other side of the ship."

"Aye, aye, raptain!" said Scooby.

Scooby steered the boat around to the other side of the ship, away from the pirate. It was getting dark, but Shaggy could just make out the rope ladder hanging from the side. He pointed at it. "There, Scoob! Jump for it!"

As they neared the ladder, Shaggy and Scooby jumped from the boat.

They grabbed the rope ladder and held on tight. The small boat sank quickly behind them.

"Come on, Scoob. Let's find the others," said Shaggy. They quietly moved up the ladder and climbed over the side.

CHAPTER FIVE

BELOW DECK

Deep inside the ship, Fred, Velma, and Daphne snuck down a long, dark hallway.

"I think I have this mystery solved," announced Fred.

"Already?" asked Velma. "How is that?"

"I bet this is one big joke by my so-called friend, Greg," replied Fred.

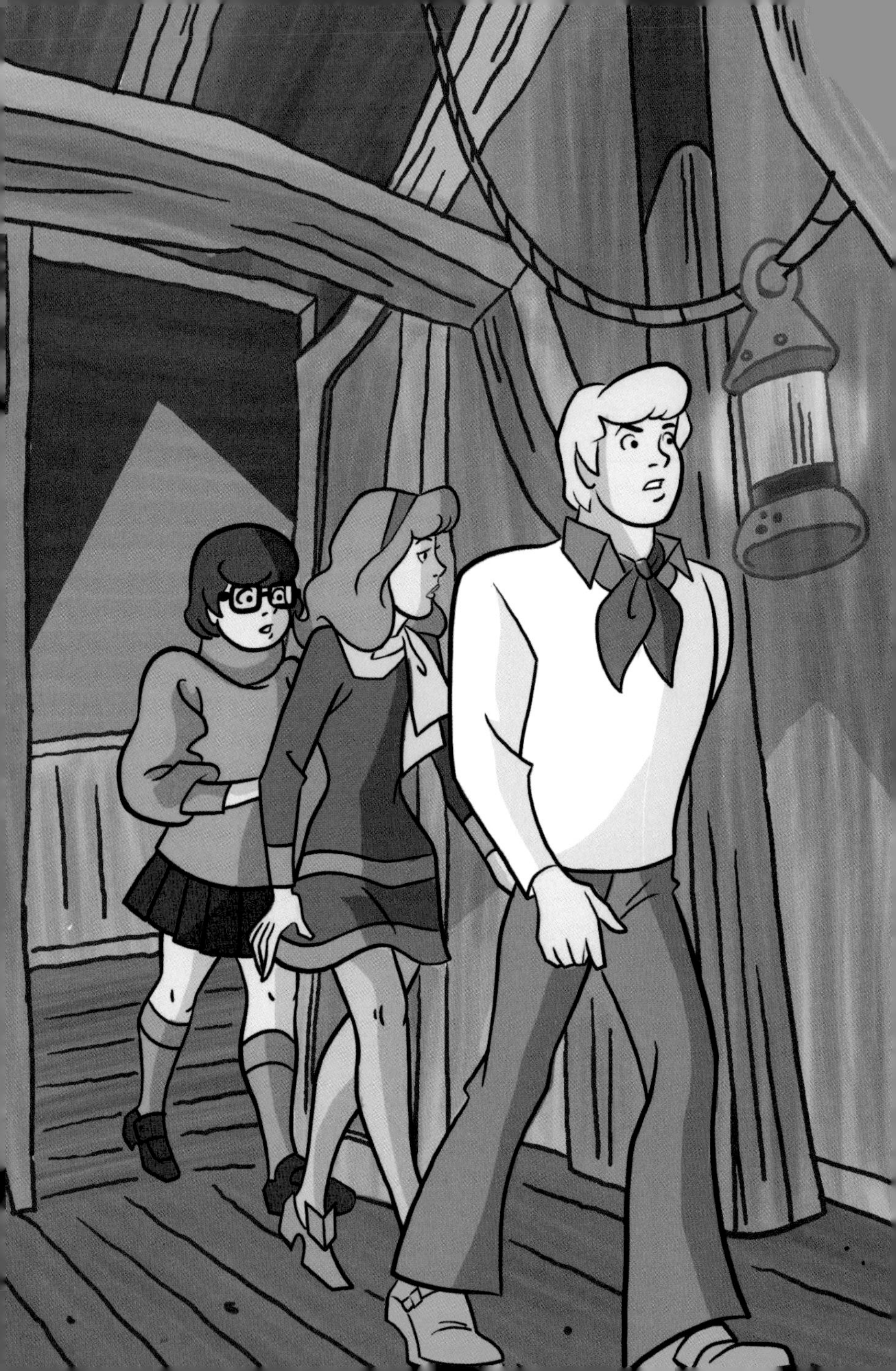

"You really think so?" asked Daphne.

Fred nodded. "He always liked to play all kinds of *pranks* on people when we were younger."

"That's why he didn't tell you what kind of ship this really was?" asked Daphne. "And why he cut the ropes tying the ship to the dock?"

"Probably," admitted Fred. "I bet it was just a way to get us to help him fix his ship."

"But why would he dress up like the masthead of Captain Grimm?" asked Velma.

"Because he knows that we would want to solve a mystery," said Fred.

Velma looked up at the work lights lining the hallway. "What I want to know is why the lights are so dim all of a sudden." She pointed to one of the bulbs. "The bulbs are glowing, but they're hardly putting out any light."

"I'll bet it's so everything looks real spooky down here," said Fred.

Daphne shivered. "Well, it's doing a good job."

Fred frowned. "I tell you, I'm going to set my best trap yet."

Daphne pulled ahead. "Then let's follow this hallway to the other end of the ship," she suggested. "We can go up on deck from the other side and sneak up on him."

"Great idea, Daphne," said Fred. "Lead the way."

Daphne led the gang through the ship. They moved past the food locker, past the old cannons, and past the brig.

"Fred?" said a voice. "Is that you?"

Fred, Daphne, and Velma skidded to a stop. They spun around to see Greg locked inside the brig.

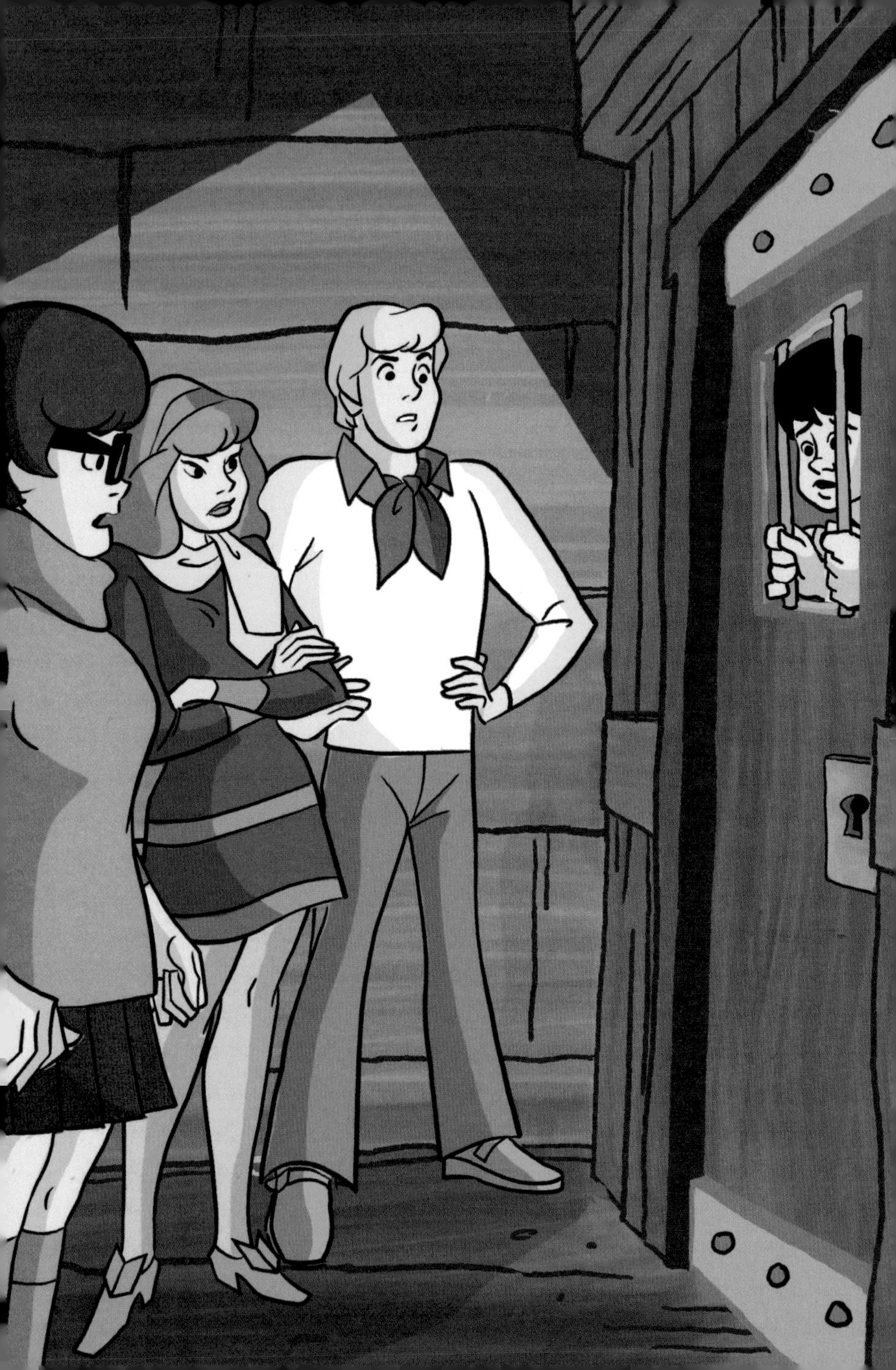

"Greg!" shouted Fred. "What are you doing in there?"

"We thought you were Angus Grimm," said Daphne.

Greg shook his head. "Not me. That spooky pirate statue locked me in here and took my key ring."

Velma tried to pull open the iron door, but it was locked tight. "Don't worry, Greg. We'll find a way to get you out of there."

"Yeah," agreed Fred. "We'll get him. After all, there's five of us and only one of him."

Greg shook his head. "Oh, no. He's not alone. He has his own crew."

"What do you mean?" asked Daphne.

Greg's eyes widened as he pointed over their shoulders. "See for yourself!"

The gang slowly turned around. Two skeletons moved down the hallway toward them. They stared with blank eyeholes and grinned with rows of bare teeth. Each skeleton held a long, sharp sword.

"Jinkies!" said Velma. "A crew of skeletons!"

CHAPTER SIX

SCOOBY-DOO RESCUE

Shaggy kept his eyes covered. "Like, you're the bestest buddy for doing this, Scoob. You know I'm afraid of heights."

Scooby grunted. "Uh-huh."

Shaggy sat on Scooby-Doo's shoulders as Scooby walked along a thin beam. The beam held a sail high above the ship. Scooby held his arms out to keep his balance.

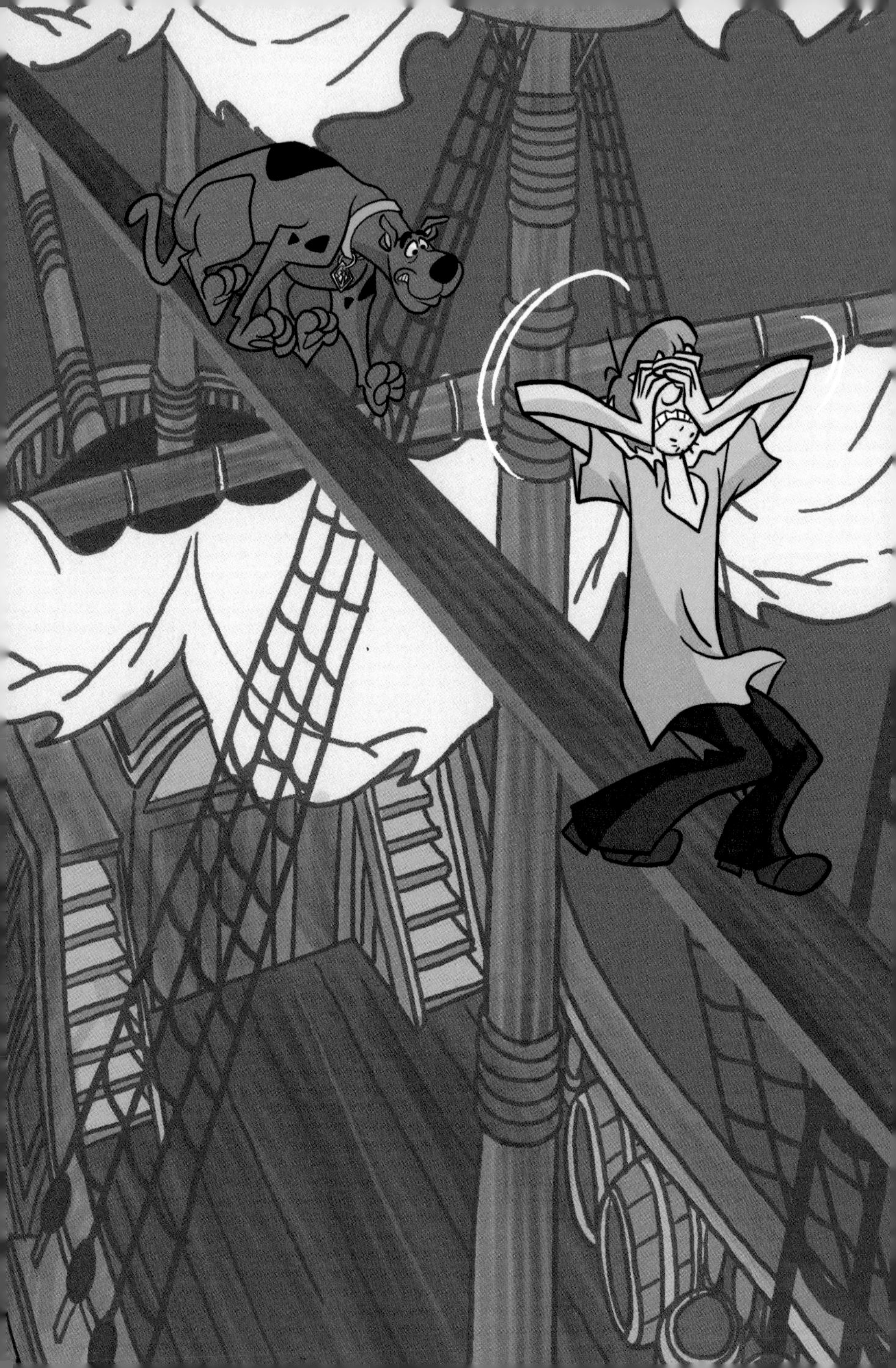

"We'll sneak across to the other side of the ship and that wooden pirate will never spot us," said Shaggy.

CLANK!

"Ow!" Shaggy yelled when his head hit something hard. He uncovered his eyes and looked up. A large spotlight hung in the ropes above them. It had a dimly lit bulb. "Like, who put a light way up here?"

"Rust don't rook down," said Scooby-Doo.

"What was that, buddy?" Shaggy asked, as he looked down.

"Ruh-roh!" said Scooby-Doo.

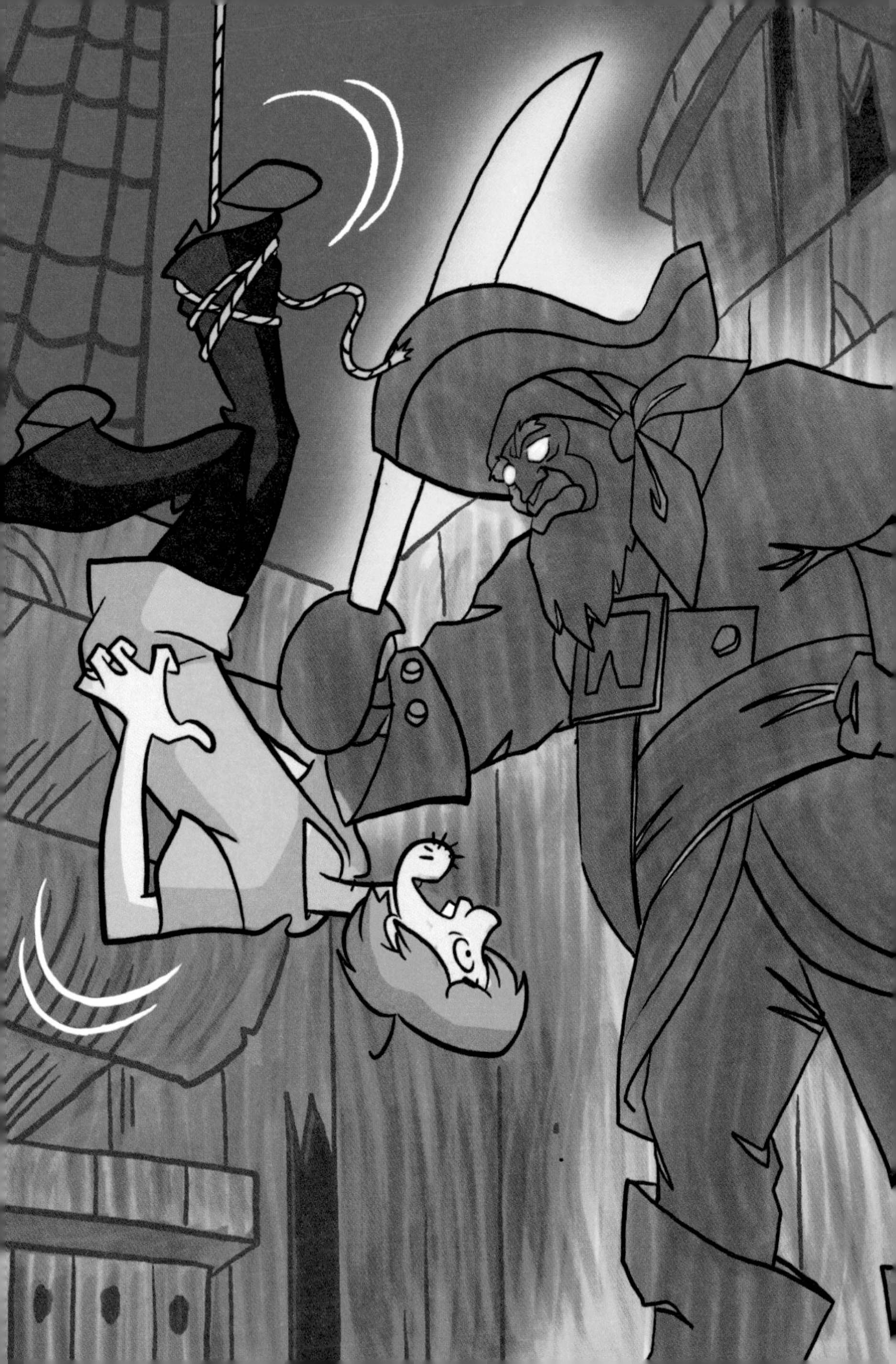

Shaggy got dizzy and wobbled back and forth. Scooby-Doo lost his balance, and Shaggy tumbled toward the deck below. Shaggy's foot snagged a rope along the way. The rope stopped his fall just before he slammed into the deck. He dangled upside down.

"That was lucky, wasn't it, Scoob?" asked Shaggy. "Scoob?" His friend was nowhere to be found. "Scooby-Doo, where are you?"

Just then, the statue of Angus Grimm stepped forward.

Shaggy gulped. "Like, not so lucky."

The pirate swung his sword and sliced the rope. Shaggy fell to the deck. *THUD!*

Shaggy got to his feet. "Like, sorry to bother you. I'll just be going now."

Shaggy tried to run away. A sword-carrying skeleton blocked his path. Shaggy tried to run in another direction but another skeleton appeared.

"Zoinks! Skeletons!" shouted Shaggy. He shivered with fear. "Why does it always have to be skeletons?"

With their swords pointed at Shaggy, Grimm and the skeletons moved in.

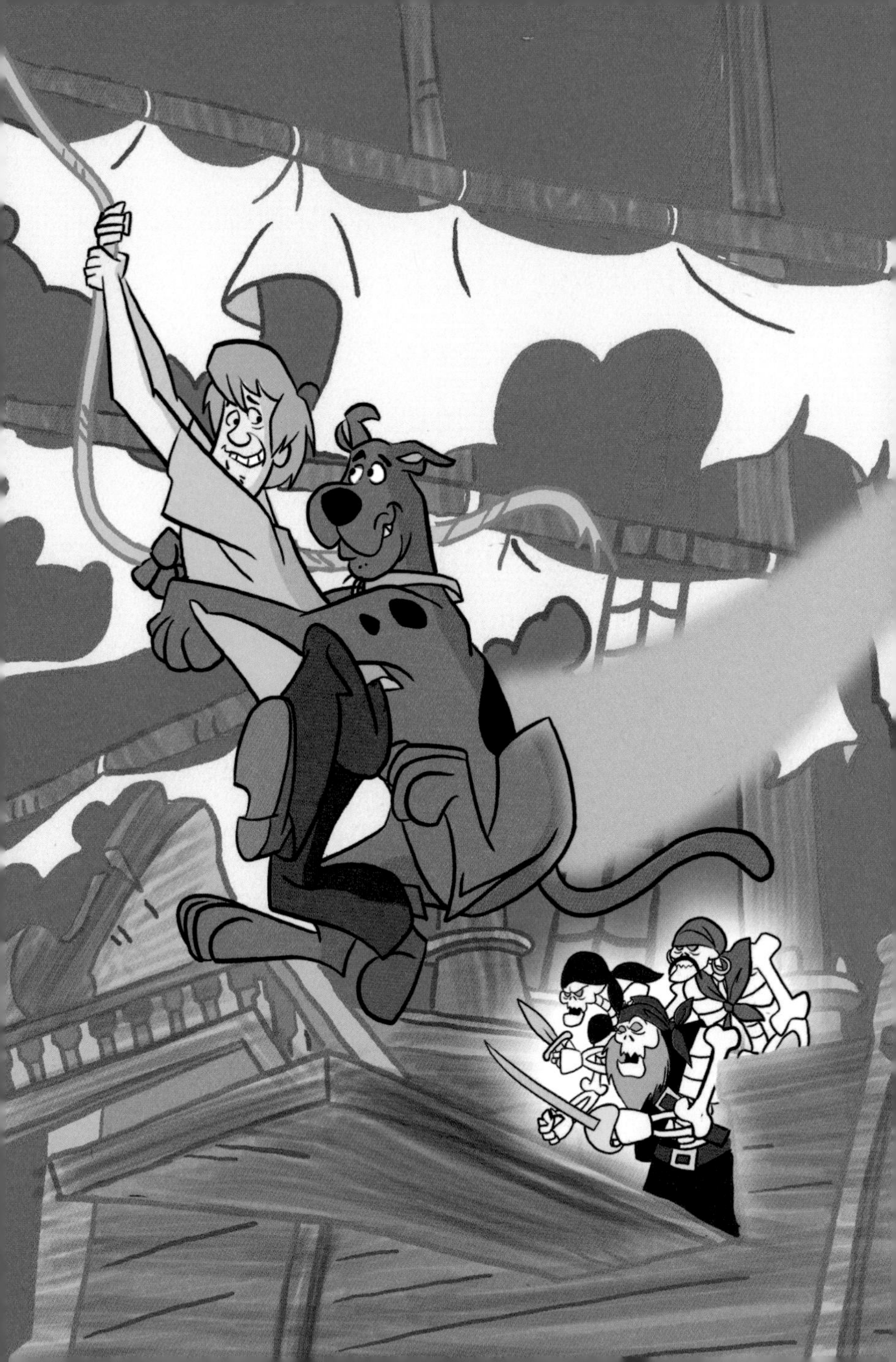

Shaggy backed away until he realized he was stepping off the ship. He stood on top of a rickety plank jutting out over the water. The monsters moved closer, and Shaggy backed farther over the water.

"Like, can we talk about this?" sobbed Shaggy. "I'm really not a good swimmer. I can barely dog-paddle."

Shaggy's feet came to the edge of the plank. There was nowhere else to go. Shaggy shut his eyes in fear.

"Rooby-rooby-doo!" said a familiar voice.

Shaggy opened his eyes to see his buddy swinging toward him.

The dog held a rope with one paw as the other reached toward Shaggy. Scooby grabbed Shaggy and swept him off the plank.

They swung out over the ocean and then back toward the ship.

"Good going, Scoob!" shouted Shaggy.

SNAP!

Scooby-Doo's rope broke. Shaggy and Scooby fell toward the deck below.

"Not-so-good going, Scoob!" yelled Shaggy.

They hugged each other and screamed as they fell. *"Ahhhhhh!!!"*

CRASH!

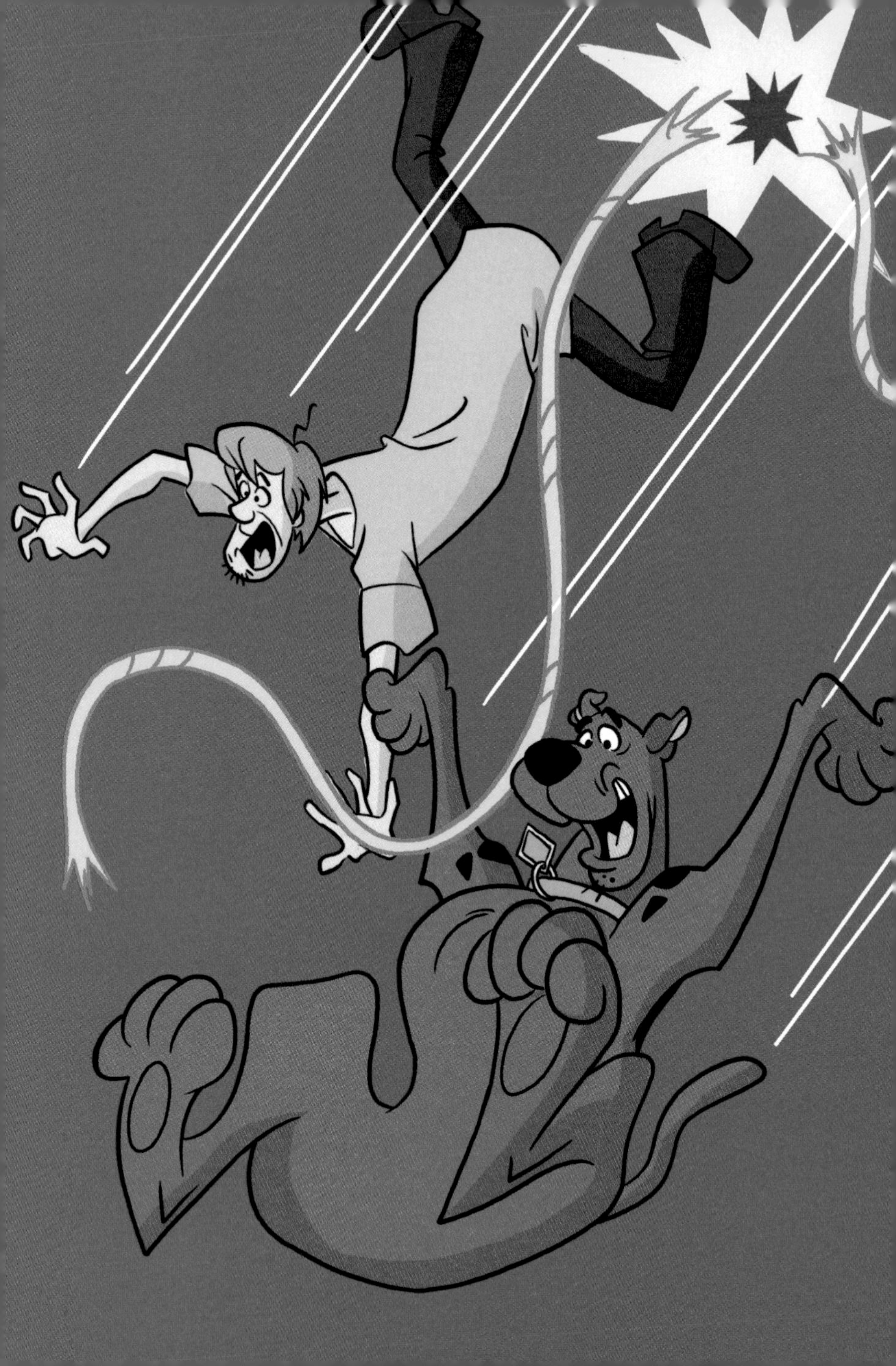

Shaggy and Scooby smashed through rotten boards and landed on the deck below.

Shaggy rubbed his head. "Like, it's a good thing we didn't fix all those rotten boards. Huh, Scoob?"

"Reah," replied Scooby.

"Shaggy? Scooby?" asked Velma.

When the dust settled, Shaggy and Scooby-Doo saw that they had landed in front of the brig. All their friends and Greg were locked in the jail cell.

"Like, what are you doing in there?" asked Shaggy.

"We're locked in," said Fred. "Angus Grimm has the keys. You have to find him and get us out of here!"

Shaggy and Scooby looked at each other and gulped.

CHAPTER SEVEN

READY, AIM, FIRE!

The statue of Angus Grimm
marched through the inside of the
ship. The key ring on his belt jingled
with every step. He frowned as he
searched everywhere for Shaggy
and Scooby.

Grimm entered the cannon deck
and continued his search. He marched
past the rows of old cannons.

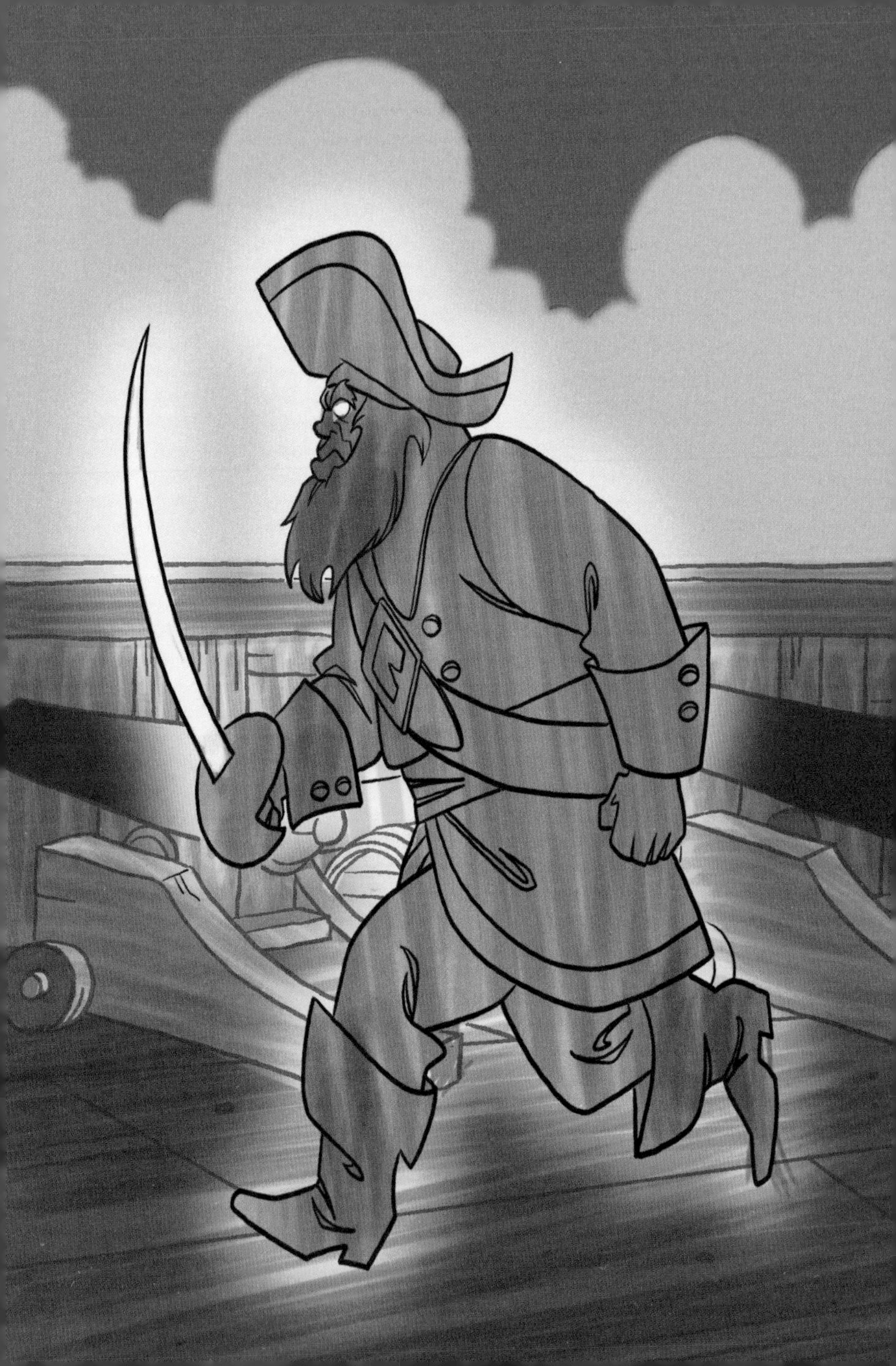

Just then, Shaggy and Scooby-Doo jumped out of hiding. They each wore a black-and-white striped shirt and a sailor's cap. They gave Grimm a *salute*.

"Enemy ship spotted, Captain!" reported Shaggy.

"Huh?" growled the surprised statue.

Shaggy pointed to one of the cannons on the deck. "Shall I ready the cannon, sir?"

Grimm grunted and nodded.

"Ready the cannon!" shouted Shaggy.

"Ready the rannon!" repeated Scooby.

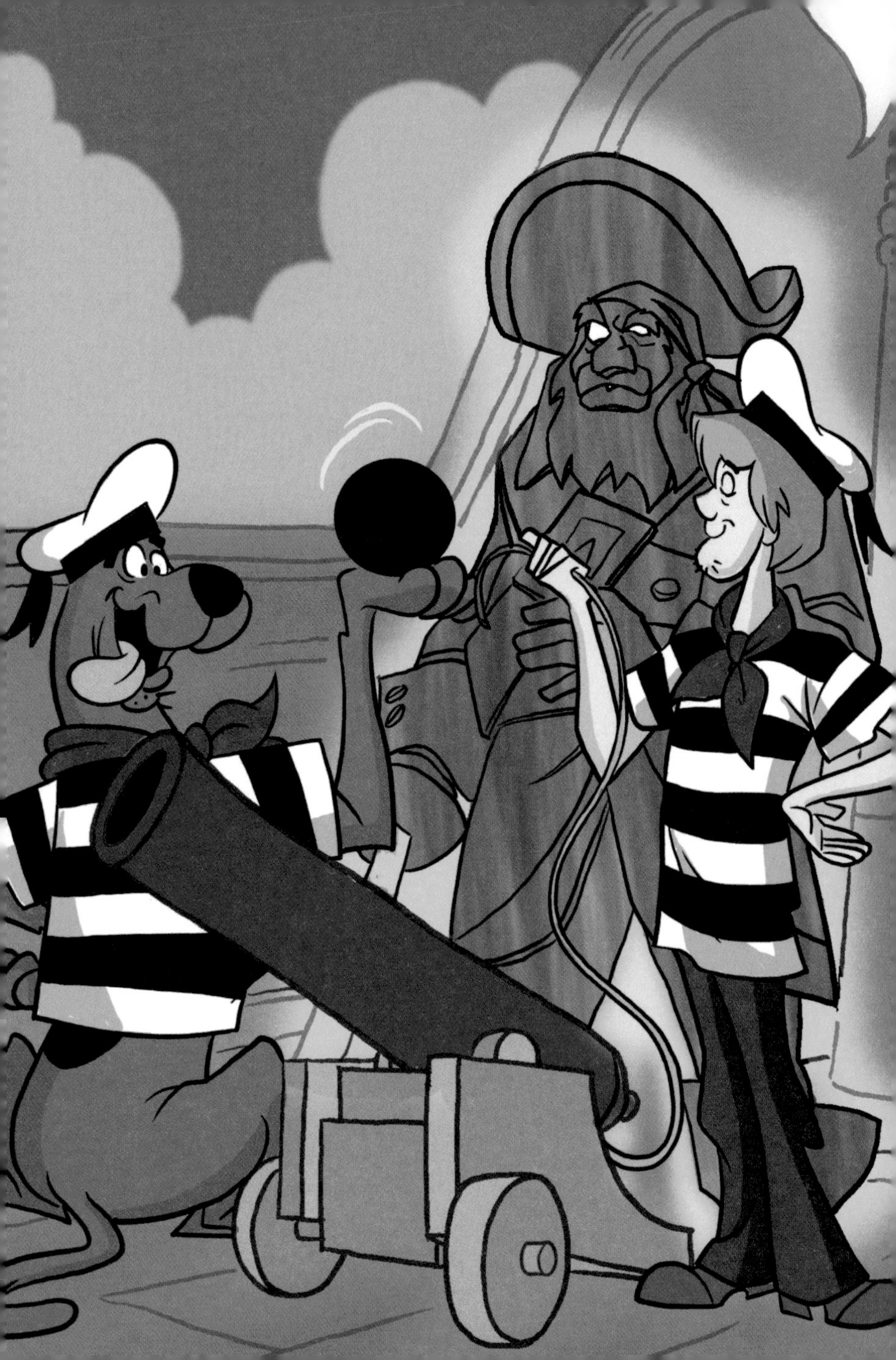

Shaggy and Scooby pulled the heavy cannon away from the opening. Grimm looked on and grinned.

"Powder!" shouted Shaggy.

"Rowder!" said Scooby. He shoved a packet of gunpowder into the end of the cannon.

"Cannonball!" shouted Shaggy.

Scooby lifted a heavy cannonball off the floor. He slowly moved it toward the end of the cannon.

"Rannon... rall!"

Scooby dropped the cannonball into the cannon. He stood back and saluted. "Rannon ready!"

"Aim cannon!" shouted Shaggy.

He and Scooby got on each side of the cannon. They aimed it left, then right, then left, then right, then left …

The pirate's head turned left and right with every move of the cannon. He growled and pushed Shaggy and Scooby aside. The statue bent down behind the cannon and aimed it himself.

"Fire!" shouted Shaggy.

"Rire!" shouted Scooby.

Shaggy pulled a cord, and the cannon fired.

BOOM!

The cannonball shot away from the ship and splashed into the water.

The cannon itself flew back and knocked over the statue of Angus Grimm. The pirate slammed into the other side of the ship.

Shaggy grabbed the key ring from the downed pirate. He and Scooby ditched the *costumes* and took off. They ran down the long hall and then skidded to a stop in front of the food locker.

"How about a quick reward before we save the others?" asked Shaggy. "Huh, Scoob?"

"Reah! Reah!" agreed Scooby. "Re rearned it!"

Shaggy found the key and opened the food locker. The door flung open, and a chill went up Shaggy's spine.

"Like, that's the scariest thing I've ever seen," said Shaggy.

Tears filled Scooby-Doo's eyes.

"Reah, reah."

The food locker was empty.

CHAPTER EIGHT

LOST AND FOUND

Scooby and Shaggy hugged each other and cried.

"I can't believe it, Scoob," sobbed Shaggy. "It's the worst thing ever."

"Rerrible," replied Scooby-Doo. "Rust rerrible."

Scooby stopped crying long enough to look back into the food locker. There was one sack left, tucked away in the corner. It was a big sack.

"Raggy, rook!" pointed Scooby.

"Oh boy, Scoob." Shaggy rubbed his hands together. They stepped inside and approached the large bag. "What do you think it is?" asked Shaggy. "Maybe it's a huge smoked ham."

"Or a rag of rellybeans," suggested Scooby. He licked his lips with his long, slobbery tongue.

Shaggy untied the sack and let it fall open.

"Zoinks!" shouted Shaggy.

Scooby-Doo jumped up and landed in Shaggy's arms. The wooden statue of Angus Grimm stood before them.

"Check it out, Scoob." Shaggy
knocked on the head of the statue.

Nok-nok-nok.

"Like, this is the real masthead,"
explained Shaggy. "Someone
must have hidden it here in the
food locker."

"A rue!" said Scooby.

"You're right, pal," agreed Shaggy. "It is a clue. Let's free our friends and tell them about it."

Shaggy and Scooby-Doo made their way toward the brig. When they got there, the cell was empty.

"Help!" shouted Velma. Her voice came from the hole in the ceiling above them.

Scooby and Shaggy quickly climbed out of the hole and into the moonlight. Once they were on the main deck, they spotted their friends.

Greg and the others were hanging above the deck in a large net. The rope that held them led down to the deck and then back up to another net.

The second net was full of all the stolen food. The food hung out over the side of the ship.

Shaggy and Scooby ran up to their friends. "Like, where are Captain Wooden-head and his creepy skeletons?"

"They're in the lower decks looking for you," replied Fred.

"Hurry and cut us down before they come back," said Velma.

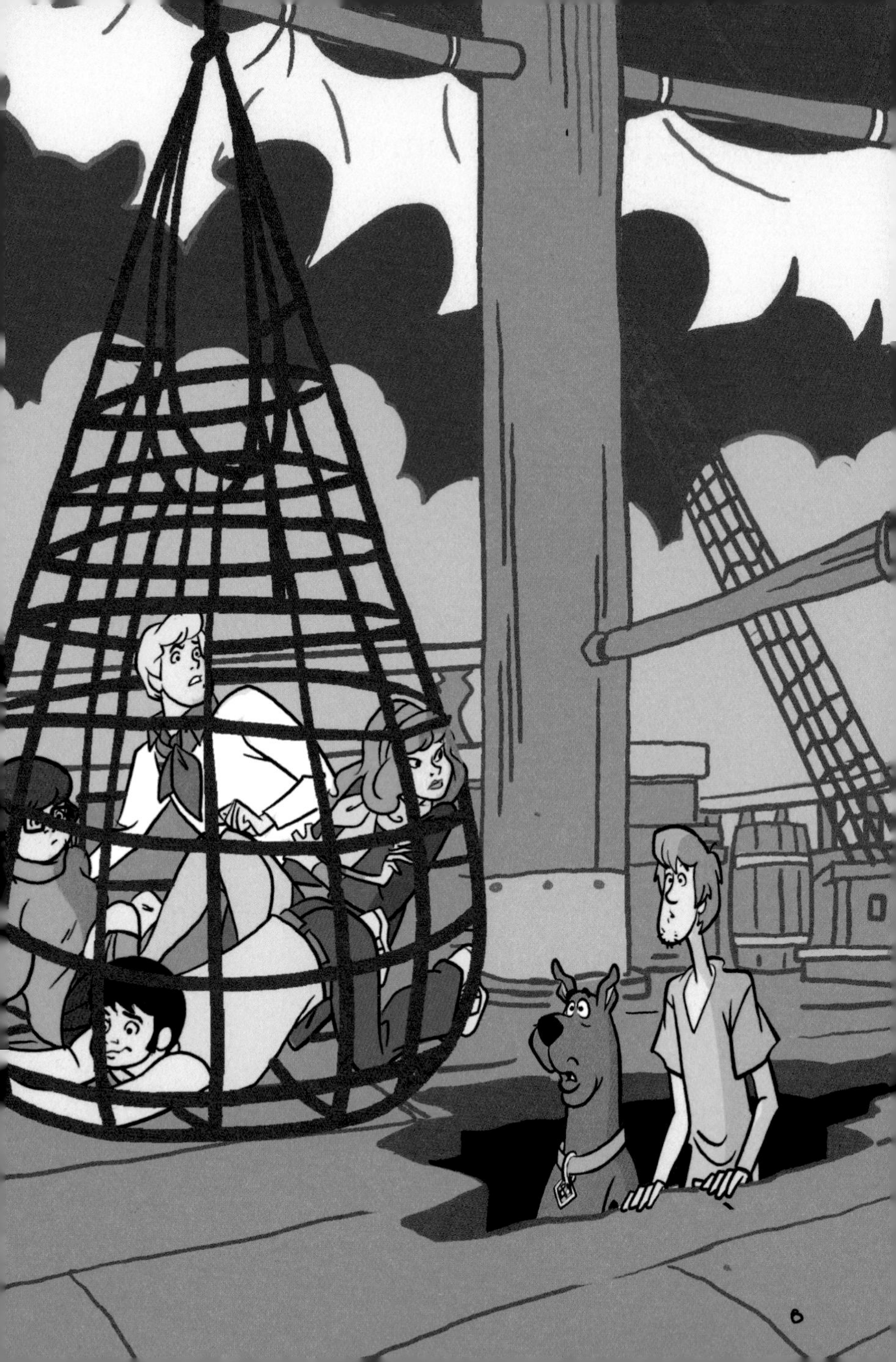

Shaggy looked from his friends to the large stash of food. "Like, if I cut you down, the food will go overboard."

"Well, who would you rather save?" asked Daphne. "Your friends or the food?"

Shaggy rubbed his chin. "Do I have to answer that?"

"Shaggy!" shouted Daphne.

Scooby-Doo grabbed a sword and cut through the rope. His captured friends fell to the deck below.

THUMP!

Then there was another loud noise.

SPLASH!

Shaggy and Scooby ran to the railing. They watched the food sink beneath the dark waves. After the food disappeared, Shaggy told the others about finding the missing masthead.

"Then I say we catch this *phony* pirate once and for all," said Velma.

Fred held up part of the rope net. "This gives me an idea for a perfect trap," he said.

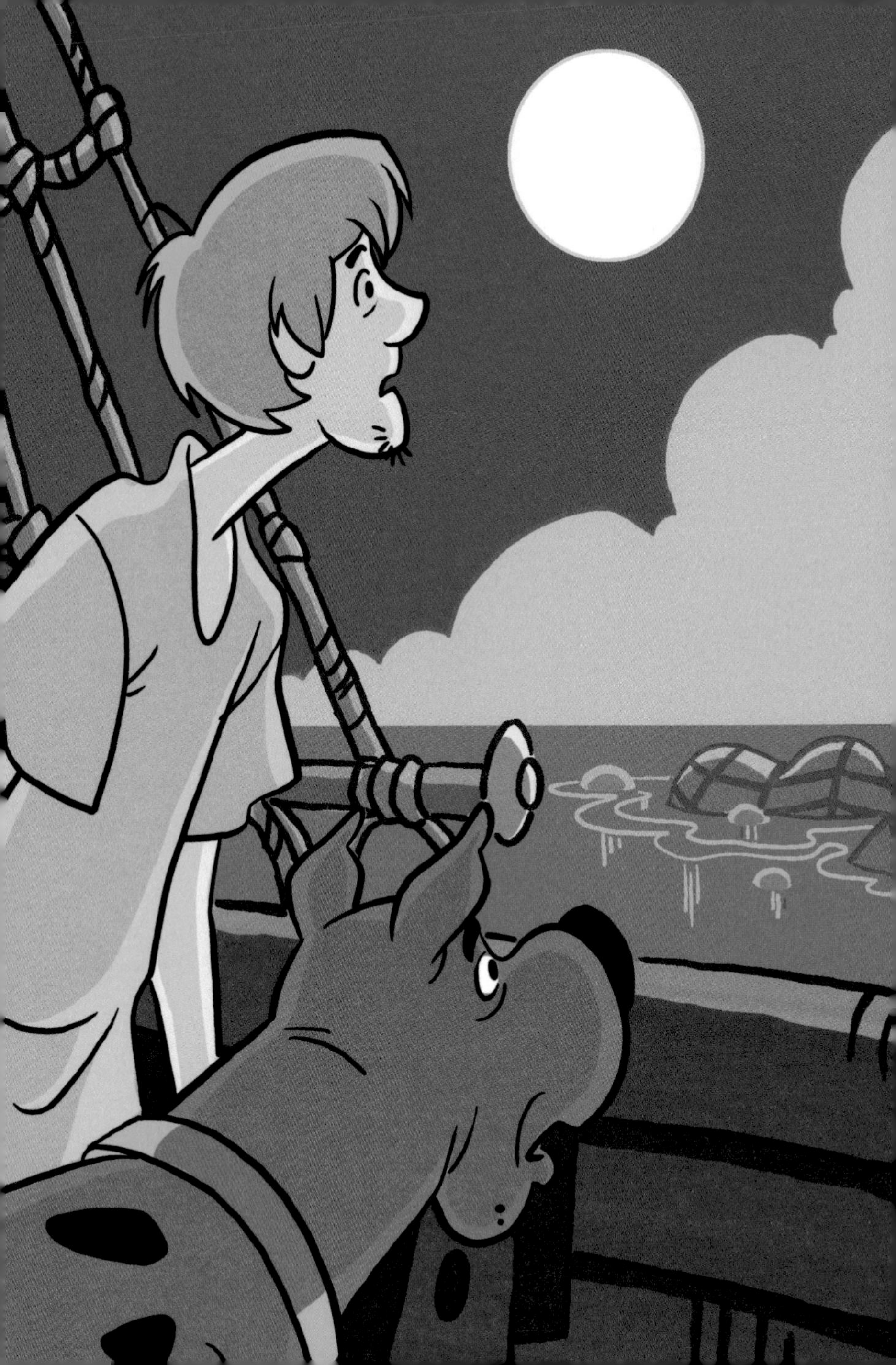

CHAPTER NINE

SWORD FIGHT

Up on the bridge, the highest deck of the ship, Shaggy spun the big ship's wheel. The giant steering wheel made the ship lean to the left as it turned.

"Ret me try," said Scooby-Doo. The dog spun the wheel in the other direction. The ship leaned to the right as the ship turned the other way.

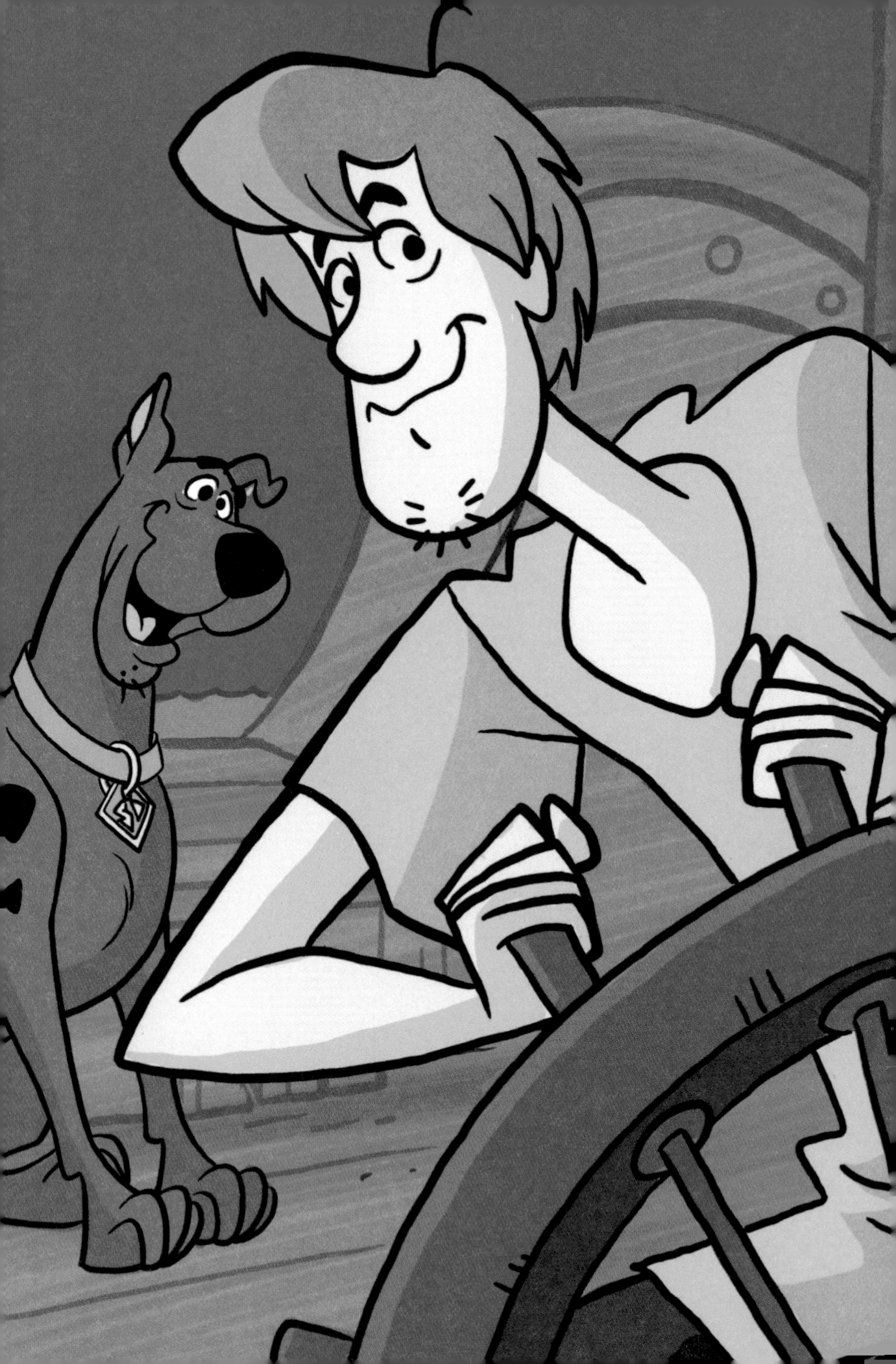

"Like, if that doesn't get them up here, I don't know what will," said Shaggy.

Scooby-Doo tapped Shaggy on the shoulder. "Uh, Raggy ..." Scooby pointed to one of the doorways leading to the lower decks. "It rorked."

Shaggy gulped when he saw Angus Grimm and four skeleton pirates step through the doorway behind them.

Grrrr!

The pirate growled at them.

"Run, Raggy!" shouted Scooby.

He and Shaggy zipped down the stairs leading to the main deck.

With the pirates close behind, they ran across the open deck. They also ran across the open net.

Once Shaggy and Scooby were clear, Fred stood up from his hiding spot. "Now, gang!" he shouted.

Greg, Daphne, and Velma each came out of hiding. They rolled heavy cannonballs toward Grimm and the skeletons.

Velma laughed. "Bowling for pirates!"

The cannonballs slammed into Grimm's feet, and he flew backward. He fell into the skeletons behind him. He knocked them all down as they piled onto the open net.

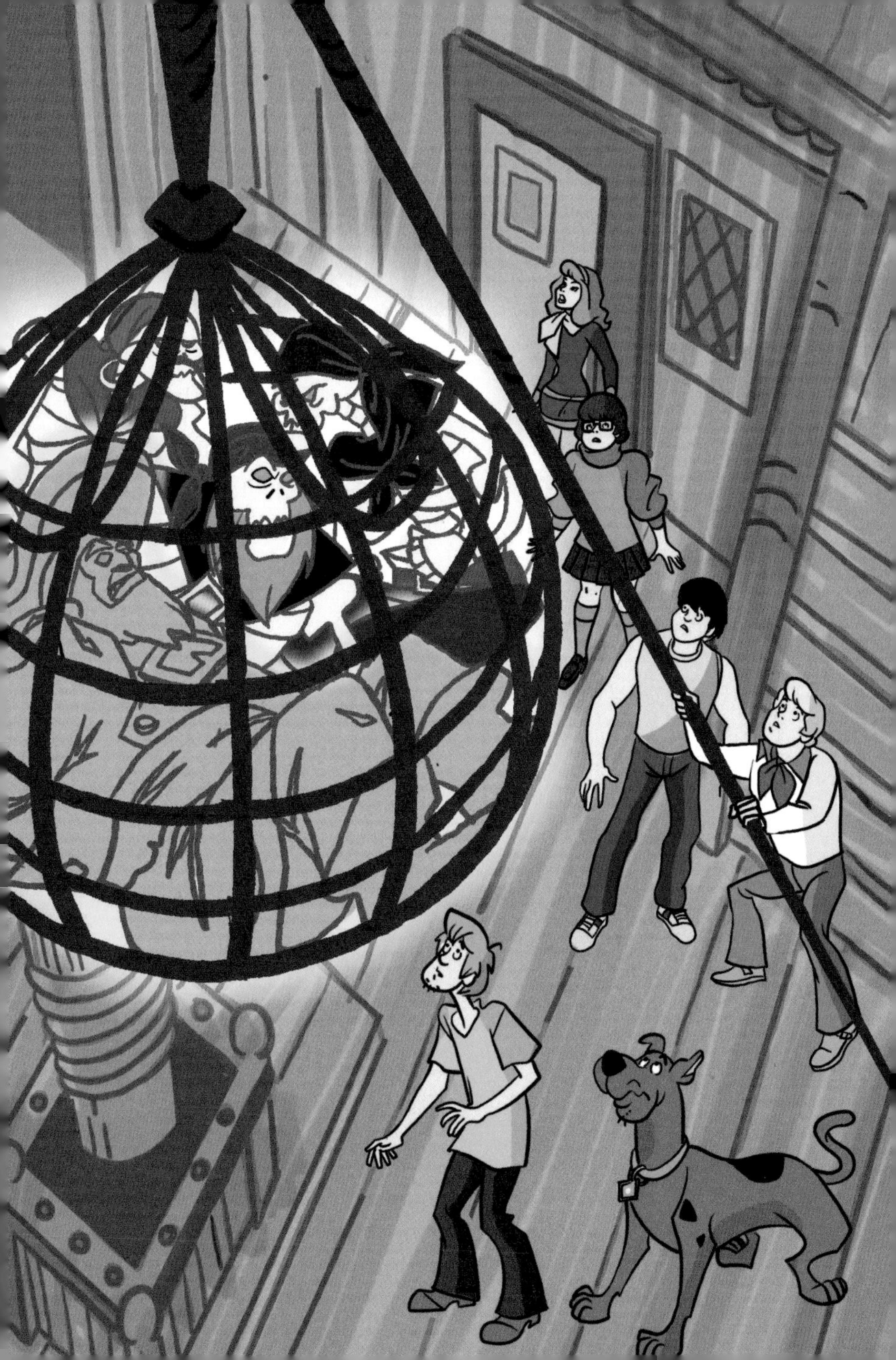

Velma pumped her fist. "Strike!"

"Okay, everyone on the rope," ordered Fred.

Everyone ran to join Fred. They pulled on a large rope. The net closed around Grimm and the skeletons. The net lifted them several feet above the deck.

Fred tied the rope to the railing and dusted off his hands. "Okay, now it's time to unmask ..."

Suddenly several swords jutted out of the trap. The pirates began cutting through the net.

Velma looked up and scratched her head.

"Fred, you did know they had swords, right?" she asked.

Fred sighed. "Yeah. Totally forgot about the swords."

The pirates cut themselves free and fell to the deck. Angus Grimm and his skeleton crew pointed their swords at the Mystery Inc. gang.

"Now what?" asked Daphne.

"Here!" shouted Greg. He ran up with an armload of swords. "We'll beat them at their own game."

The pirates charged toward them.

Klink! Klank! Klink-klank! Klink!

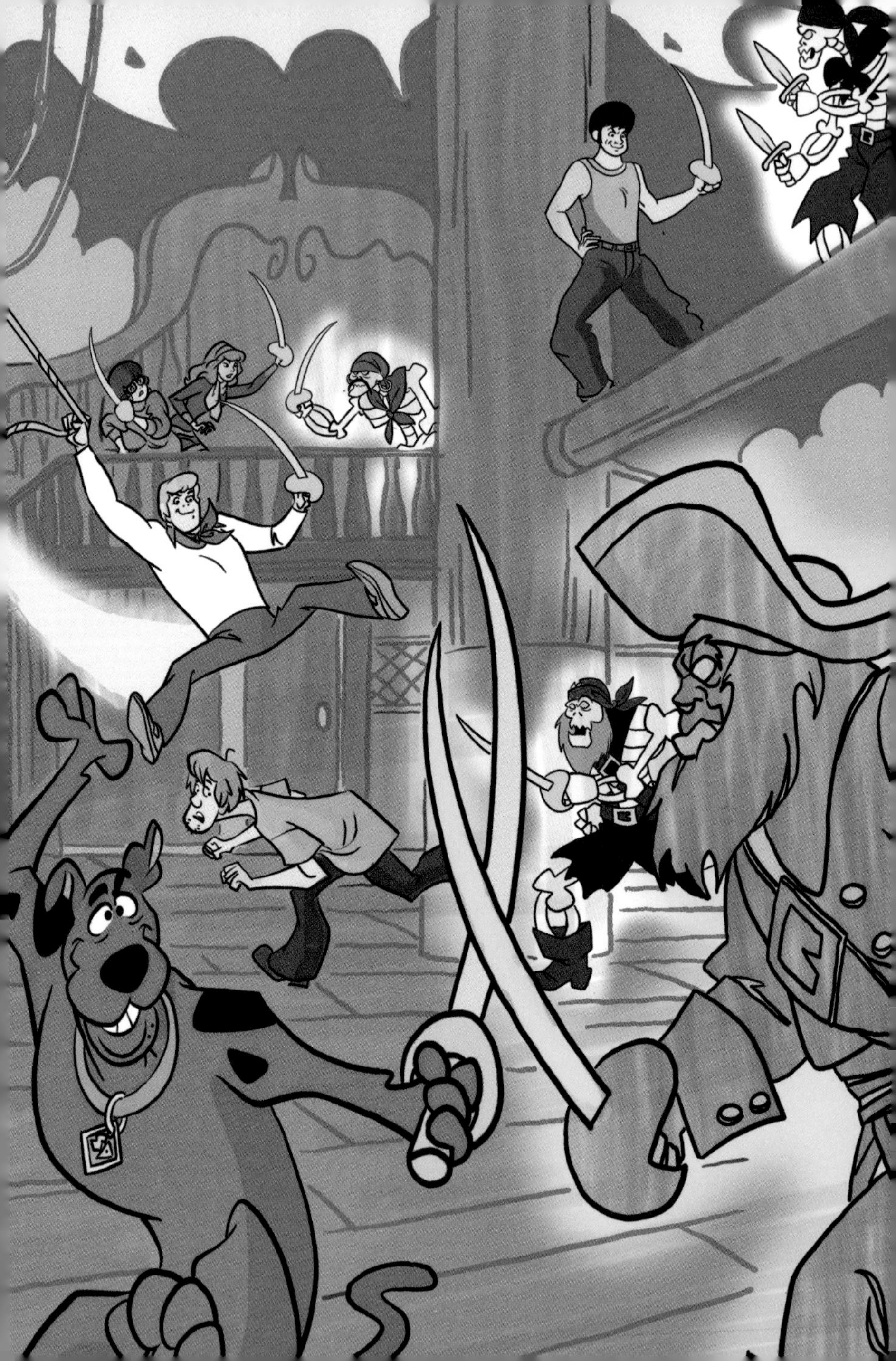

Fred crossed swords with an angry skeleton. Velma and Greg fought off their own skeleton. Daphne jumped out of the way as a skeleton swung at her. Shaggy whimpered as a skeleton chased him around the deck.

"Like, they're way better at this game than we are," said Shaggy.

Scooby-Doo faced off against Angus Grimm himself. The angry pirate struck Scooby's sword and knocked it out of his paw. Grimm swung at Scooby again but the dog was ready. His tail held another sword, and he blocked the blow.

Grrrrrrrrrrrr!

The pirate growled as he knocked that sword away too. It was clear that the pirates were better at sword fighting. They surrounded the gang and pushed them closer and closer to the edge of the ship.

Klink! Klank! Klink-klank! Klink!

The pirates were winning.

CHAPTER TEN

PIRATE OVERBOARD

Greg and the Mystery Inc. gang stood with their backs to the railing. The pirates moved in from all directions. There was nowhere for the gang to go.

"We're surrounded," said Velma. "I guess this is the end of Mystery Inc."

"We're doomed, all right," agreed Fred.

Shaggy turned to Scooby. "Like, it was nice knowing you, buddy." Scooby-Doo wasn't there. Shaggy looked all around. "Buddy? Pal?"

"Rup here, Raggy!" shouted Scooby-Doo.

The gang turned to see Scooby-Doo standing on the bridge behind the ship's wheel. He wore a large captain's hat and a long coat.

"Rold on!" the dog ordered.

Shaggy and the rest of the gang dropped their swords. They whirled around and held onto the railing. Scooby-Doo spun the ship's wheel as hard as he could.

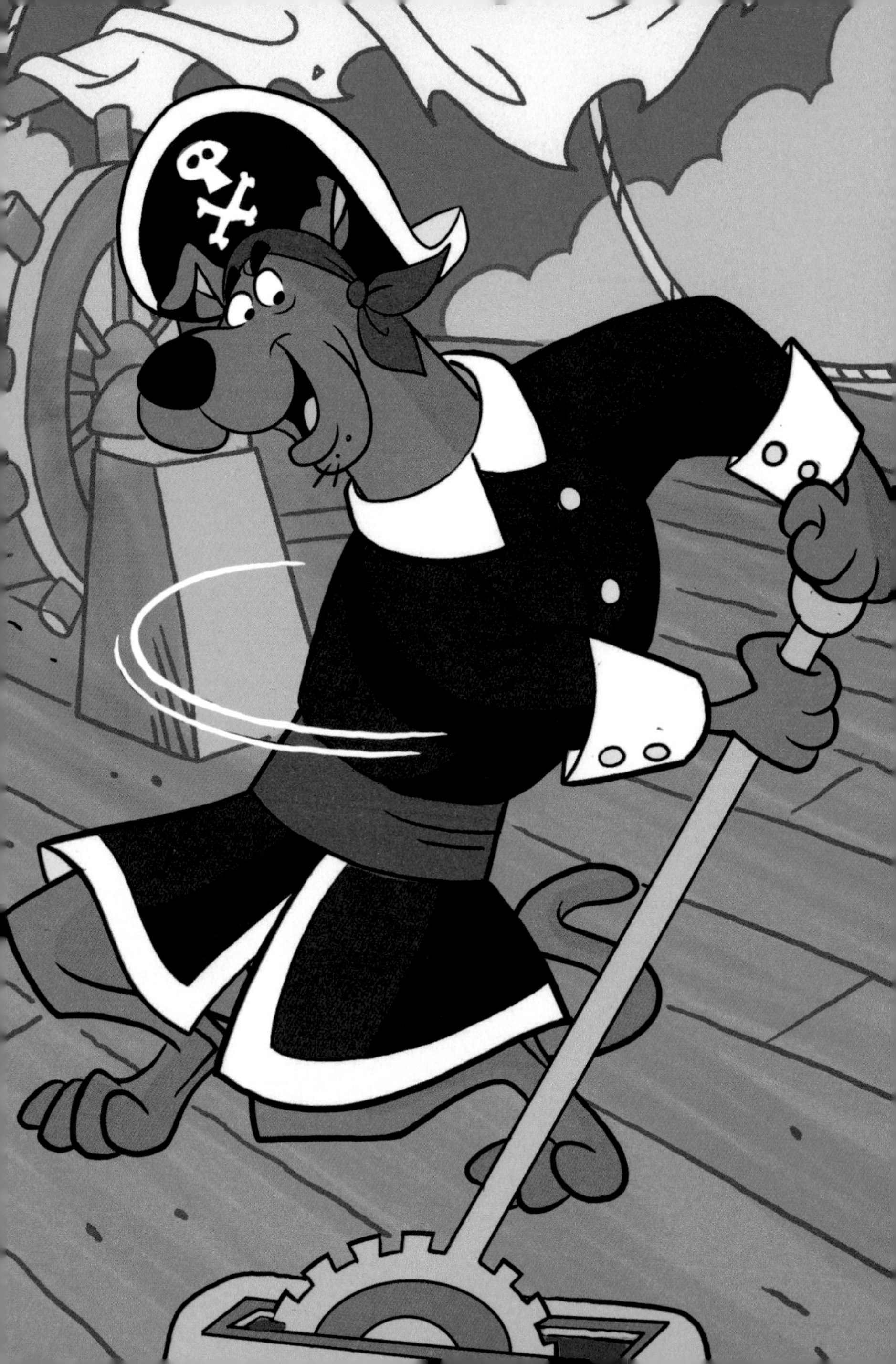

The ship turned hard and tilted up on one side. The skeletons fell to the deck and slid across to the other side.

Grrrrrrr!

The statue of Angus Grimm growled. He slowly climbed uphill toward the helpless gang. Just then, a loose cannonball rolled under his feet. The pirate lost his balance and slid across the deck with the skeletons. They all flew over the side and landed inside a hanging lifeboat.

"Rooby-rooby-doo!" Scooby shouted as he pulled a *lever.* The smaller lifeboat dropped to the ocean below.

SPLASH!

Everyone rushed to the side of the ship. They looked down to see Grimm and the skeletons piled into the small boat. The boat floated next to the big ship. A thin rope kept it from drifting away.

"I think it's time to unmask the bad guys," said Velma.

Grrrrrr!

Angus Grimm growled up at her.

Shaggy picked up a small cannonball. "I learned a new trick today," he said. "Like, do you want to play cannonball catch?"

Grimm shook his head. "Okay! You win! You win!" he shouted.

Each of the skeleton crew removed its mask. It turned out that they each wore a tight black mask with a white skull painted on the cloth. Grimm removed his mask too. The younger man underneath looked a lot like the angry pirate.

"How did you know they were wearing masks?" asked Greg.

"The first clue was the weird light bulbs all around the ship," explained Velma.

Shaggy pointed up. "Like, there's one up there in the sails too."

"Those are called black lights," continued Velma.

"They only put out a little bit of light and make everything look creepy," she said.

"But they also make white things look as if they're glowing," added Daphne.

"So the skeleton crew were just men wearing tight, black costumes with skeletons painted on them," finished Fred.

"But the biggest clue was when Shaggy and Scooby found the real Angus Grimm masthead," said Velma. "That meant that someone was running around pretending to be the masthead come to life."

Greg leaned over the side. "So, who are you, anyway?"

The man in the Grimm costume frowned. "I'm Duncan Grimm. Angus Grimm was my great, great grandfather."

"So, what are you doing on my ship?" asked Greg.

"Well, when I heard about your floating museum idea, I had to put a stop to it," continued Duncan. "And I would've done it too … if it weren't for you nosey kids."

"But why wouldn't you like an Angus Grimm museum?" asked Fred. Duncan shook his head.

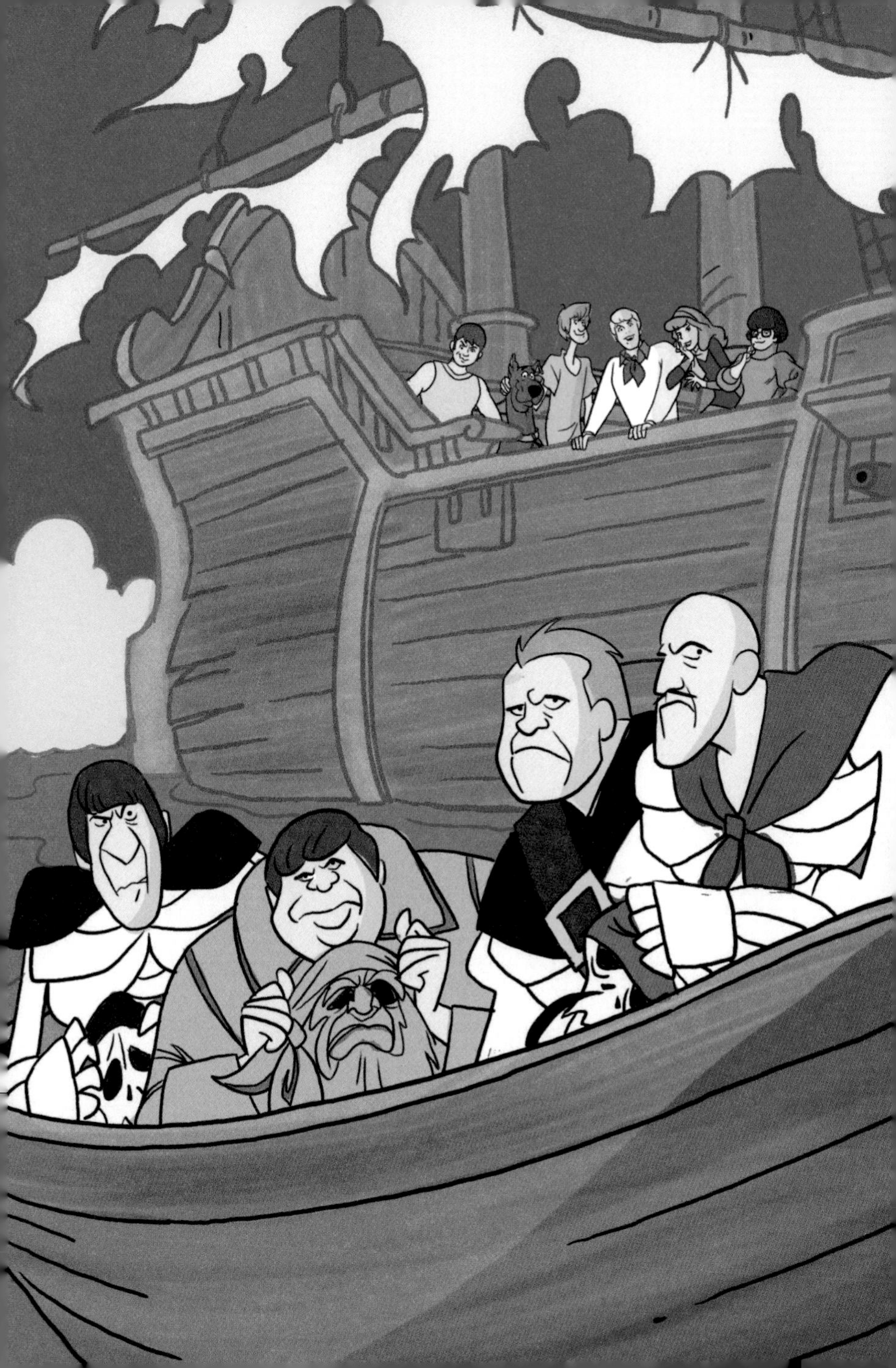

"I didn't want any more shame being brought to the family name. It's bad enough having a name like Grimm," said Duncan.

"Well, you're staying put while we sail back to land," said Greg. "We'll let the police sort this out."

Greg turned back to the others. "Is everyone ready to set sail for shore?"

"You bet," said Fred.

"We're going to need a vacation to rest from this vacation," said Velma.

"We can't go yet," said Shaggy. He and Scooby wore full diving suits with tanks, masks, and flippers. They walked over to the railing.

"Like, since all our food is sitting on the ocean floor, Scoob and I are going to dive down and get some snacks."

Greg laughed at Shaggy. "Don't worry, guys. Like I said, Fred told me all about you. That's why there's a whole other food locker full of food."

Fred put a hand on Greg's shoulder. "That should at least hold them for the trip back." He turned back to Shaggy. He looked around. "Shaggy? Scooby?"

Shaggy and Scooby-Doo were already on their way to the second food locker. All that was left was a pair of empty diving suits.

THE END

ABOUT THE AUTHOR

MICHAEL ANTHONY STEELE has been in the entertainment industry for more than 24 years writing for television, movies, and video games. He has authored more than one hundred books for exciting characters and brands, including Batman, Green Lantern, Shrek, LEGO City, Spider-Man, Tony Hawk, Word Girl, Garfield, Night at the Museum, and The Penguins of Madagascar. Mr. Steele lives on a ranch in Texas but he enjoys meeting his readers when he visits schools and libraries all over the country. He can be contacted through his website, MichaelAnthonySteele.com

ABOUT THE ILLUSTRATOR

SCOTT JERALDS has created many a smash hit, working in animation for companies including Marvel Studios, Hanna-Barbera Studios, M.G.M. Animation, Warner Bros., and Porchlight Entertainment. Scott has worked on TV series such as *The Flintstones, Yogi Bear, Scooby-Doo, The Jetsons, Krypto the Superdog, Tom and Jerry, The Pink Panther, Superman,* and *Secret Saturdays,* and he directed the cartoon series *Freakazoid,* for which he earned an Emmy Award. In addition, Scott has designed cartoon-related merchandise, licensing art, and artwork for several comic and children's book publications.

GLOSSARY

COSTUME (KOSS-toom)—clothes people wear to hide who they are

HAMMOCK (HAM-uhk)—a hanging bed made of canvas that is tied between two posts

LEVER (LEV-ur)—a bar or a handle used to work or control a machine

MUSEUM (myoo-ZEE-uhm)—a place where objects of art, history, or science are shown

PHONY (FOHN-ee)—not true or real

PLANK (PLANGK)—a piece of wood that holds something in place

PRANK (PRANGK)—a playful or mischievous trick

PROPELLER (pruh-PEL-ur)—a rotating blade that moves a vehicle through water or air

SALUTE (suh-LOOT)—to give a sign of respect

STATUE (STACH-oo)—a model of a person made from wood, metal, or stone

TATTERED (TAT-erd)—old, torn, worn, or falling apart

VESSEL (VESS-uhl)—a boat or a ship

WATERCRAFT (WAW-tur-kraft)—boats and ships collectively

DISCUSSION QUESTIONS

1. Scooby-Doo got to spend some time at sea. Would you ever live on a ship? What would you like about it? What would you not like about it?

2. Captain Grimm's ship was named The Salty Dog. Can you think of another good name for a pirate ship?

3. A living statue of a pirate is pretty creepy. What kind of scary monster will Scooby-Doo and the gang face next?

WRITING PROMPTS

1. The Mystery Inc. gang didn't get the vacation they expected. Write about something that happened during your favorite vacation.

2. Pirates are known for liking buried treasure. Write about how you might find some buried treasure.

3. Fred's trap didn't go as planned. Write about how you would trap a ghost pirate.

LOOK FOR MORE

SCOOBY-DOO!

BEGINNER MYSTERIES